I0543570

A Copley Novel

Written & Created
by Clifford Jones

ISBN 978-1-9162544-0-4
Meaningless Mud Publishing

To Lara

Inspiration
Dedication
Belief

☐

Copley

UNDER the SOD

By

Clifford Jones

Chapter One

Fuck. Copley.

Bugger.

Fuck.

What a fucking mess.

Why.

I mean why here?

Why me?

Fuck.

Just what you need.

One body slap bang across the section. Not a gaunt skeletal remain, a bit of femur shining back in the drizzle; an empty eyed skull with a   toothless grin "Hello I've just messed up your day, I'm waiting to be exposed – just when you wanted to get down to what you consider to be the interesting bit – I get in the way and bugger it all up for you".

Ohh No. Not a quick heyho with the wooden spatula, quick tidy up; photo "Now smile please, let's have all those bones all measured and dusted clean, have you looking your best"; then gracefully removed with all the reverence of a bag of spuds. This was no "next please" this was a pain in the arse".

No easy way out on this one.

Fuck. Copley, old son, we have a dirty inconvenience, a mute reminder of our sliver of breath and its dirty terminus.

A full blown not very dead corpse; podgy flesh held in by a Marks & Spencers mac.

Not any old mac; a Marks & Spencers bloody mac.

Sod it; where's my mobile; here goes the rest of the week for nothing. Another fine mess.

Sod it, sod it. Fuck.

"Police. Copley, Professor C o p l e y. I'd like to report finding a dead body."

Copley had not enjoyed the call, every word was another hour of not getting on with the job. All he wanted was a nice clean excavation, to get down to the late first century settlement of Portsea. A world where the vibrant Roman port was going through massive expansion; where the shopkeepers would have vied for the troops attention, the bars overflowing and the sights sounds and smells from the bath houses and brothels would broadened the mind to the limit; all of the Roman empire would be passing through its new streets and colonnades.
No.
All the delights and mysteries of past were on hold, delayed; whilst the petty events of the present cut deep into the narrow excavation timetable.
Copley stood and observed.

The primary skill in archaeology, standing and looking. But more than that knowing how to look. The difference in colours and textures, the way the earth gives up the past.

Copley was not amused. Some fucking bastard had dug into the past, disturbed it and left a carcass in the bottom.

The very thought of the first police car bearing the joyous and expected news of a forensic team on its way created the instinctive reaction in Copley an urgent need for a pint, or several; however this was prevented by a string of questions as to why he was digging a hole in the middle of a field in Cumbria.

Copley had answered. Archaeologists did that sort of thing. That, as a result of LIDAR and GPRS there was an anomaly in this corner of a field forever Cumbrian and based on other researches it was worth a poke around to see what was going on.

The poking around didn't normally involve dead bodies, or if it did, they had been long beyond the attention of the Cumbria Constabulary.

A fleet of cars, flashing lights and vis vests huddled within a self -imposed blue taped corral.

Copley's first body; had been in very similar circumstances. The corner of a field in Hampshire, one sunny summer in 1972; where was it now? Paris Corner, Newham. Vindlonus A temporary Roman fort, or possible Mansio, found by means of the then experimental resistivity survey equipment. To be precise the finding of its corner, thus worthy a bit of a dig – bingo a dead body still fully clothed with finger prints all over the blade still in its lithe back; one girlfriend that got more than she ever contemplated along the verdant tunnel like lane up to the site.

The boyfriend had planned it well; kitchen knife, new from Woolworths in Farnham; shovel in back of car; pick cheating girlfriend up, high hedged lane; go for walk, stab her at edge of field shaded by hedge, saving valuable time and effort; good deep hole and easy digging- deep against the badgers and foxes; finish job neatly and go back to pub for a celebratory pint. Corner of a field in the middle of nowhere – no one would find her; other than a bunch of archaeologists.

The best laid plans of mice and Ford Cortina MK II drivers with shovels in their boot.

Got life for it.

The knife was in as deep as the handle.

Copley got the chance to exhume the remains.

Copley remembered the Inspectors words

"You gentlemen are the best we could possibly ask for. Get her out in one piece."

With a casual dexterity the small team had set about the task. Copley remembered the looming figures of photographer and an inspector above the body, intruding on the task.

Afterwards he remembered hearing a conversation regarding his age – he was just thirteen. Nobody had minded at the time; Copley looked forty from the age of ten. It was an introduction to the primeval nature of decay, the degeneration of the self; the passing of life by whatever means – it meant something, or nothing. His instinct was investigation; his drive was how and sometimes why. He'd done a good job that sunny day, others had commented on his maturity and dedication to the task; he hadn't been shaken by the scene. A pint of beer was reward; the police sergeant had slapped him on the back and offered him a fag. He'd mastered the art of digging the dead out of the sod; inching back the enveloping earth, plucking the suppuration free from the cold clawing earth around, the sun above; the darkness of the trench; life dragging death back into the light, a resurrection rather more than an exhumation; a very satisfying business.

"Always talk to them as if they were your patient"

Copley told his students, that the dead deserved respect. He didn't always believe his own rhetoric. The dead were often in the way; just as the corpse in Newham was in the way of Cortina man's plans, this corpse lying in a field in Cumbria was his inconvenience. A dead stop.

Copley jerked his mind back to the business at hand. He was, if nothing else, an archaeologist and archaeologists can cope with anything, especially with a pint in the hand.

"Always set up your headquarters in the nearest pub; a place of warmth and comfort; you will save yourself valuable time and effort if you listen to the locals. The pub has the telephone and you can soon get the Landlord to get plenty of Gin in."
Mortimer Wheeler

Police methods had changed since the 1970's; the Portsea trench was ideal from a forensic point of view. The clomping of size 14's in gumboots had been replaced with flat soles encased in paper overall bodysuits. The body, only partially exposed required two side trenches being dug across either side of the section. Copley had agreed to let his post grads assist the forensic team to release the body; his intent, as ever, directing, rather than digging. Forensic teams were oft as not from an archaeological background or at least respected the arts nuances and techniques.

Copley changed his mind; he was not prone to doing so, unless he was persuaded by a higher power, normally clad in shiny black leather, or in stark contrast a publican pulling one for the road. For once the desire for a pint was gone, something from the past, half fascinated, half disturbed him; an opportunity to regain some missing sensation perhaps but also the desire to enquire. He could mask his inquisitiveness by suggesting it was his duty to look after his students. He should lead as he was ultimately responsible for all he surveyed; and anyway he had always held the view that archaeologist should never direct others to dig up the dead.

"Archaeological exhumation: it is the individual's right to refuse on religious, or ethical grounds. No adverse action should be taken against a person for so refusing"

A pure invention, an excuse to be in on the action; as his students were ever willing to get to grips with the task of shoveling bones out of the deck at a rate of knots – in all his years of digging he had never heard of a single refusal. One more skilled hand in getting down to the body was useful, there was plenty of soil to shift; the forensic team had positively supported his request to assist as the detective inspector, understood the nature of the task. Along with five of his students he had begun the slow but sure process of reaching the rest of the body.

Copley stood looking. Looking long. Looking deep.

"Archaeologists are masters of observation.

Copley was a master of the art. For art it most definitely was, no science can begin to understand the relationship between the archaeologist's sense of touch taste and smell, combined with an eye for the unusual. Anybody can look, but an archaeologist will see, based on their understanding of the whole environment around them and the research of place. That is an art, not a science. The archaeologist is the gatherer. The billboard of humankinds' past.

Copley gazed beyond the seen World letting his mind to run free, observing and recording without preconception, without prejudice, without confines; yet holding a rein of thought strung along a true consistent path.

Or, as Copley was oft to remark

"Perusing the subtle lenses laid down by humankind and having a good guess along the way."

Copley gazed, then with his mind fixed, he subtlety lowered himself to the trench.

Down into the earth, the disturbed earth; an earth shattered by a spade digging frantically down; slicing the earth, deep; savage cuts. The sides of the grave dug for the corpse revealed a frenzied series of slices along its edge; digging a grave by hand to six foot depth requires a ladder or at least two earth steps down to allow the digger to work; the spoil going over the shoulder at the last, or laboriously bucketed out. Whoever had dug this grave had worked fast; suggesting someone of considerable agility and strength – there was only evidence of one large step down into the depths.

Copley's intervention had revealed the woman's shoes; two red shiny pinnacles appearing as his trowel had scraped the loose surface. Copley had instinctively reached for a paintbrush to ease the soil away; stopping himself and using an evidence bag first, just in case the soil was not a match for the surroundings.

The red shoes; they glistened. Copley had drifted into his own private world. Hardly private; his women all had one thing in common; tall, long legged and well shod. Copley was a leg man; a primeval desire for a thigh booted temptress which he fell for every time. A very public private passion that was oft open to exploitation – Copley was fully aware and couldn't care less. It wasn't as sordid as some.

Copley's reflection showed the edge of a grim smile across his face- gone in an instance as he shadowed his work. He was enjoying himself.

Such care and attention were a present day reality, he hadn't been so precise in the 1970's. Cortina man was caught by simply leaving his fingerprints on the knife in the girls back and having a criminal record prior to his deed. A tempt of fate too far.

Copley was concentrating, an instinctive passion as deep as the earth – a need to understand to excavate and do it well, putting the pieces of life back in place. That's what he was good at and of course theorizing when the bits were missing, or not fitting his view. A natural thing to do, to want to put the world into a personal focus, a means of coming to terms with reality – create one's own. The difficult part was always to get others to agree with it; especially those with the money.

Copley had continued to clear the earth from around the shoes. The rest of the team had by now revealed the remains of a face, a crusted blood black mess of a face, with a frazzle of blonde hair otherwise a dark red black solid mass. A heavy impact had taken the upper jaw nose and eyes and pushed them back into the brain, taking the front of the scalp and skull down into the brain; a large hammer, a sledgehammer size blow; but not enough to stop reconstruction of the remains. Copley noted the mac, Evelyn his secretary, confident and passionate, had one like it; the buttons dull brassy and mostly for show; Copley had muted that if anyone needed a mac wouldn't it have been more use if it actually did up. This had fallen on deaf ears; the whole idea being to wrap the belt tightly; again, not using the buckle around ones waist, just as the corpse was dutifully applying. No need for a mac now; nice and dry under a plastic tent with an attentive audience to the latest fashion accessory – a bloody useless mac.

The mac belt appeared to be holding the body together, the body fluids had not wholly departed a good old stew of decay was rising that stuck at the back of the throat; so much for face masks. Skeletal remains never gave this amount of bother although Copley could remember an instance in his past when they did.

He had managed to kiss a mummified corpse once, he tripped over a finds tray on a dig in Guildford. Copley had always carried a few pounds so landing on the ground, it gave way; it being only a crust over a coffin top. The soil and timber unable to withstand the weight Copley had found himself in intimate embrace with the remains of an ex resident. It had raised quite a laugh at the time.

The shoes.

Copley hadn't really taken notice of the shoes on the girl at Newham; women were another land when he was thirteen; he'd learnt every inch of the territory, charted passages, delved deep into the hinterland since then, but still didn't really understand where he'd been. But shoes he knew well; women and shoes; they liked shoes. Those shoes looked new, shiny and new; not cheap; no wear at all.

A perfume of decay, yet fresh, skin like putty, where it was exposed, and not remodelled with a sledgehammer. Death melting to the earth drip by drip. Purifying and anonymising.

Copley had rested up, sitting watching the team continue the task; he'd drunk a cold black tea and had felt utterly detached; strange; normally he would have been in command and wholly opinionated. This time he had simply gone into a professional trance; a place of solace; there was something very wrong about this. Not just the fact it was a fresh corpse; something beyond that – it was really very annoying, but there was something else. Instinct told Copley to beware. There was something very wrong here.

He hadn't noticed that two of the students had dropped out of the team; the remains of the face, the smell had overtaken their keenness. Copley was oblivious to all that. He'd just wanted to see the body out of the way, far away.

And out of the way it was; photographed measured and gently slid sideways onto a lifting rack; the ground beneath leaving an impression of its recent absentee.

Copley had wondered if that was the only mark this poor broken form would have on this earth, a slight indentation on the soil of Cumbria. That, at the end of the day was all we were going to end up as; a small indentation or ashes on the wind. Copley cared less as long as he had his pint; the warm thighs of a good woman or three and a comfortable academic roof over his head tomorrow, such thoughts could go to hell.

Copley snapped back to reality; his private thoughts locked back in the cupboard; his students needed him, it was not just unprofessional not to have noticed, it was just plain bloody stupid of him. Whilst they were post grads they were still green to life and this was a pretty stiff lesson. He should have noticed; he cursed himself. Why was this body; no, not this body, the Newham body getting to him? Newham was in his thoughts; perhaps it was a trauma. Perhaps because it was his first; perhaps he had forgotten how frightened he had been; but he hadn't been. He had got stuck in with vigour; his detachment – that was the lesson, long learnt and badly understood. He had been brave. He wanted to be part of the team, to face stark truth. It had left a bloody smear indelible upon him. But enough of sorrow. Bury it beyond the pomp and bluster
Such feelings would have to wait. Wait a very long time. Copley hoped he would never be given the chance of remembering.

"Ernie can you take charge for a couple of hours, I better have a word with those that found the body; first time for this sort of thing. Whatever the Inspector and the forensic lads say goes. Ok? Where are they?"

Ernie White; Copley's site supervisor, confidant and drinking pal duly nodded, flicked his head to the right, meaning the pub.

"Rightho"

Copley felt suddenly alive again, stepping away from that trench, out of the tent into the daylight, away from the body that was interfering with his dig; getting in his way and messing up his timetable. Copley's head turned from introspection to role of master of his artful veneer and pretence, of care for his fellow man. The mantle of the Professor of Archaeology; the man that held theories that proved to be right in the face of his detractors; the man that, never let anyone forget his achievements, his triumphs; his importance – he was it, he made sure he was it.

Truth for Copley was stark. The folly of a man that wholly relied on his secretary Evelyn to keep his academic empire afloat and Ernie to make his digs run like clockwork; the man that that had passion for imparting knowledge; yet found students a confounded nuisance; his colleagues, (unless they agreed with his views) as no more than petty creatures that kept his department afloat by attracting research monies that he would plunder at every opportunity. The man that ruled with an amiable pomposity that people found infuriating and if they crossed him, deadly; the man that reveled in his power with a sociable consummate political flair.

Copley made his way to "The Fulford Arms" with one thing on his mind, a pint or two; the students wouldn't keep him long. It had been intense work in that tent; thirst provoking indeed this might be an afternoon session if he was lucky. Ernie, as ever could keep everyone happy. The female student that had found the body was going to be in a bit of a state - understandable, a very harsh lesson in savage death; but potentially a good one. The blessed Evelyn would make sure she was back at her 'digs' surrounded by attentive curious fellow students – a bit of celebrity status would take away the angst, the shock of putting your trowel into that mess. Pity she got the headfirst. The rest would have been nothing – a buried bag of smelly rags; anything; not the face. Understandable shock that. Still, she would soon have more important things to think of; getting a job in the real world.

What's a body without a face in comparison with that?

Copley dragged the heavy sprung door back and walked into the comforting atmosphere of the Fulford Arms, the smell of chips wafted through the air; a row of hand pumps and a bar; what finer sight was there? He saw the two post grads sitting on the far side of the pub, deep in conversation. The landlord instinctively pulled a pint of Yates for Copley and duly added it to his tab.

"Bit of fun up at your dig I see"

The Landlord was waiting for the whole scenario to come out; Copley was bound to tell him. The local bush telegraph was eager for news of the body. Copley felt obliged to assist in this task, but took a good quenching swig of Ale before starting. A little dramatic build up never hurt. A lesson he had learnt from watching Hitler – make them wait, longer, longer still and then when they are about to give up, you give it to them straight between the eyes. Expectation is everything with an audience, however small.

"Nasty business; it's a female; I would say in her mid twenties; face completely smashed in. I assisted the forensic team to exhume her. No idea who she is, no identification at the moment; nothing in the way of clues . Getting in the way of my dig, which is a bloody nuisance; our bodies tend to be a bit older than this one.

I would have expected this place to be crawling with journalists?

"Can't get here; phones been going mad; I've taken it off the hook. Really nasty accident up at the junction; nothing can get in or out of the village. Three fire engines up there; multiple job; so unless they decided to catch the train or helicopter into the village nobody gets here and none of them would have the nowse to catch a train, you mark my words there'll be a bloody helicopter on the car park at this rate. Might as well be; nothing else on it."

Copley's glass was empty, the beer not touching the sides; washing away the past few hours as it went. A refill duly poured.

The post grads could wait, Copley's spirits were lifting, as he walked from the excavation to the pub he had been looking forward to a few interviews, possibly a bit of TV. This was annoying. At which point his thoughts were interrupted, as a policeman walked into the bar.

"Professor Copley? Mr Tricker said we'd find you here"

"Yes officer, I've just popped down to see the two post grads over there; they found the exhumation hard going"

The empty glass and the third of a pint in the second offered the police sergeant a slightly different interpretation of Copley's presence, but his task was more abrupt.

"Hanna Kemp; she's one of your students?"

"Yes, she found the body. That's her over there with her friend"

"I'm afraid to have to inform you Miss Kemp died in the road traffic accident at the top of the hill. There's been a pretty horrendous accident up there; road's still blocked. Multiple casualties, Miss Kemp's car seems to have exploded."

Copley was blank, stunned. Wasn't one of these two in the bar Kemp?

The sergeant continued.

"There was nobody else in the car; just Miss Kemp"

Copley was, for once in complete shock; a student's death was always messy for the University and the departments reputation and ultimately his career. Within him there was the academic relief that there was only one student dead, it could have been worse, although there were a number of students, indeed a bus load that he would have happily seen being given a lift by Ms Kemp, as long as he personally wasn't responsible for them.

"Hanna was in no fit to drive a car after she found the body; terrible state."
One of the students piped up.

Copley turned towards the two post grads, they in turn were staring at him and the sergeant looked as if he was siding with the students. All their faces were pale, unquestionably, hostile; spiteful faces meant trouble for Copley.

A silence persisted; broken after several lost breaths by the sergeant's radio sparking into life; a garbled voice enquired if the Professor had been found.

"Yes, I've found the Professor. You were right, he was in the pub."

The Landlord refilled Copley's glass; Copley having finished his second pint whilst the sergeant answered the radio.

"Did either of you two know Hanna?"

The sergeant called across the bar to the post grads; they had made no attempt to move from their seats. An air of quiet defiance, animosity; especially towards Copley that the sergeant could see only too well, pervaded. Copley wasn't going to get a chance to act as intermediary, no chance of him protecting himself in this arena.

Sipping his beer quickly Copley could concentrate his thoughts as he stared into the amber depths of his glass. He certainly couldn't remember ever seeing Hanna, other than for the briefest of moments, whilst Ernie had taken her out of the trench in a distressed state. He certainly had never seen her in one of his infrequent 'chats' with the students. These were mere ticks in the appropriate boxes that Evelyn organised; quick cup of coffee and be pleasant for ten minutes before herding the spawn of the devil back to their holes in the ground. Unless they had good legs and turned up in boots; then he wouldn't have the foggiest. Just another blur that kept in a style he demanded.

Copley was suddenly beginning to feel queasy, a childhood dread of the unknown; that turning the handle, that all too real shadow in his bedroom wall, isolated. Where was Evelyn when you needed her? This was going to be nasty; questions would be asked, this could be bad in high places; least she wasn't dead on his dig, but she was one of his diggers. Thank God it happened elsewhere the HSE would have a field day; at least this blessed Hanna lass had been wiped from this mortal coil without getting her entrails on his section. Somebody else dropping bodies on him was fair enough, an accident; fate; so, a clean record. Dead students, it happened all the time, drink, drugs, suicide. Suicide, perhaps the sight of the dead girl had sent her over the edge, and she had deliberately run her car into the nearest HGV?

"Hanna was a mature student; I saw her occasionally, she took an ancient history module, she was a second year. She lived out at Sandynog. Had her own car; there was a boyfriend I think."

One of the postgraduate broke the ice relieving Copley by supplying everything he didn't know of Hanna. Copley was relieved; the sergeant could concentrate on her, whilst Copley considered what best to do.

"Excuse me officer, I need to ring the University. I take it nobody already has?"

Copley excused himself as the sergeant went and sat with the post grads. Fumbling for his phone Copley glanced at the screen, catching his own reflection; he was pale, but he was alright, nothing had happened that could possibly be pointed at him. He was still in command; he was an Archaeologist he could do anything; he could certainly cope with this. A mature student had mangled herself into an HGV; nothing to do with him. How mature? He hadn't noticed any students in their forties around the place, not that he took much notice of anyone. He needed Evelyn; she would sort this all out.

The mobile lurched into action, after a pause the familiar tones of Evelyn arose out of the confusing ether.

"Copley what's going on over there?"

"Bit of a problem, Evelyn"

"It's never a bit of problem with you Copley. You have a body I believe?

"How did you know that?"

"Students have phones unless you hadn't noticed. Actually, Ernie rang me this morning, filled me on the details; that will keep the gossip mill going here for a while. Come on, what do you want me to do?"

"It's the other one."

Copley was perfectly calm. All was well, he could talk to Evelyn. Evelyn would put it all in its place. Neatly tidied away, filed, dispatched and destroyed as she saw fit.

"What other one?"

"One of the students. Hanna Kemp got herself wiped out in a car crash a couple of hours back. She was the one that found the first body. Thing is Evelyn, I have the Police here asking about Hanna and the Post Grads know more than I do. I'm in a bit of a spot. You know what I'm like with students."

"I know exactly what you are like. Hold on and I will look her up; you don't deserve me, you really don't."

Copley waited as he heard a click of a keyboard.

"Hanna Kemp; aged 36; studying Joint Hons Archaeology and Ancient History; course tutor Julian Smith, the weasel; second year, looked good for a first; next of kin; boyfriend at 127C Sandynog Lane, same address as given for her. We have a photo and her file; I'll send it across. She was an active member of Archsoc, held a full HGV licence, obviously that would have made her popular for trips. Hang on, yes she seems to appear in the Student Union records; assistant Transport Officer; recently been to Germany; that enough for you.?"

"Thanks Evelyn send it to my phone, and I expect the Police will need it; the detective I was dealing with was Garry Henderson, Cumbria Constabulary, but I suspect it will be someone else as it's a traffic accident. At least I won't look a complete prat when they ask me about her. You will look into this for me, won't you?"

"Just give them the file, you always look a prat. Anything else oh great lord and master?"

"This looks as if it's going to be difficult; the body in the trench is bad enough; if it wasn't for the road being blocked this would be mayhem right now. Better inform the Vice Chancellors office"

"I already have. This is going to look good isn't it? The student that found the body ends up a corpse herself within hours. Odd that. But that's co-incidence – well, let's hope it is?"

Copley thought for a moment, was it the case, as he'd considered, that the girl had panicked, made a mad dash to get away, straight into a HGV.
"That's the problem Evelyn; did she panic after she found the body?"

"Well you should know. But you don't because you got Ernie to do it, didn't you? Ernie has as much emotional attachment to the human race, as an amoeba, unless he's drunk then all he wants to do is get students knickers off. You, stupid idiot I cannot believe you left her in his tender loving care! "

Copley dutifully kept quiet until the tirade calmed itself. He knew the form.

"Actually, after the initial discovery I inspected the body as best I could and rang the Police. Ernie acted very professionally as I would expect from any member of my staff; he got the students away from the immediate scene; they are all co-operating with the Police. I have been contemplating how best to put my report to the Vice Chancellors Office and the Press Office, which you will no doubt deal with in your own inimitable way. Staff and students acted in an exemplary manner and we will continue to do so. Actually, my dear Evelyn, it was a very bloody mess, face smashed in with a sledgehammer, or something of the sort; messy and it hadn't been in the ground long; the smell wasn't too brilliant, you get the picture"

He was back on form; the panic had passed the cut throat with a smile academic was emerging from its lair. Evelyn knew how to flick his switches and get him back on track

"Surprises me that somebody didn't pick the smell up before they found the body?"

Copley's mind went back to Newham; had he remembered a smell? Whilst the smell of rotting flesh is one that once inhaled is never forgotten, the memory plays tricks; he couldn't remember the smell, that sunny day in Hampshire. Had she smelt he was close; yet he couldn't remember?

Copley let the question pass: he really wasn't sure; nobody had mentioned smell.
"Love and kisses; speak soon"

Copley pushed the red button. It was good to be alive. Evelyn would sort everything. All he had to do was be his normal self; any sign of compassion and caring would look as false as hell. Ernie would play his part; sturdy Ernie, at least when sober. Evelyn would be waiting for him at home. Long legged Evelyn with lots of surprises for him.

Back in the pub Copley saw that the sergeant seemed deep in conversation with the Post Grads; Copley had a new pint glass, full and waiting for him. What an excellent Landlord. All would be well.

At which point Detective Henderson strolled into the bar and headed straight for Copley.

"Professor Copley, can you tell me anything about Hanna Kemp?

Copley's mobile buzzed and the goddess Evelyn poured forth the files via a SMS file.

Copley waited until the message was complete and turned slowly towards the voice. Copley looked at the phone and back to Henderson.

"Good afternoon Inspector Henderson. At Castletown we take very great care of our students; this is a tragic loss, terrible, quite terrible. I have organised for Hanna's file to be sent to you, and if I am not mistaken it has just arrived. Here are Hanna's details, do you have Bluetooth, or should I have my secretary forward it by other means I am, of course at your disposal? There appears to be no direct family, a boyfriend, I have no exact details. I wasn't present when Hanna found the body, it's a big site. I did examine the body after she was taken out of the trench, I mean the corpse; Hanna was looked after by her fellow students. Much better than a fusty old Professor don't you agree?

Henderson, as far as Copley was concerned, was no threat to him; they both had their territory and Henderson seemed grateful for the extra forensic hands. Henderson was hardnosed, but Copley's approach, as intended, tilted him off balance

"Thanks. If you can hold a minute, I will pick your phone up. Yes, that's ok; got it. Any problems and we can get it from your Secretary. She's just rung me; how she found me I have no idea; she's very efficient."

"The best"

Copley liked to crow about his prize bird; even when she was giving him a sizeable kick up the rotund arse; which he thoroughly enjoyed; especially if she was in spiked thigh highs.

"Thanks for lending us the students for the body retrieval; they look a bit shook up; the forensic lads will be down in few minutes; they'll see them right for a pint; the rest of your students are fine. You have a good lot of students. How did Hanna fit in, her being a mature student?

Copley decided on a straight bat; here came the first ball, heading straight at his wicket.

"I'll be perfectly frank. I have no idea. If for instance she had been caught sleeping with six of my fellow colleagues at once, then it might have reached my ears as idle gossip; or more seriously missed three lectures on the trot; then I might have seen her, or at least past her in my office. Otherwise most students are distant beings. Education has become a machine; I just fuel it with money that I beg off corporations, multi nationals and the like and in return I tell the Government that standards are getting better all the while. I'm sorry I know nothing. You're better off talking to her peers; your sergeant seems to be getting somewhere."

Copley was taking Evelyn's advice, he always did. It meant survival, it meant stability; wise Evelyn; he couldn't do without her. Copley knew she had him exactly where she wanted him, and he really didn't mind; especially when he woke up in the morning and she was there; he wasn't alone, and the World always felt good.

Henderson walked over to his sergeant. Copley didn't matter; he relaxed and reached for his pint. He never really mattered, only when it came to 'fronting' his department, only when he was protecting himself and that was all there was.

Henderson joined the post grads. A happy little bunch of nobodies thought Copley trying to put a picture of Hanna Kemp together; and they wouldn't be any the wiser just sitting talking about the peripheral, the ephemera, the gossip. Would the Police find out anything? No. They could surmise that Copley was an uncaring bastard not in charge of his students, that was true; but Copley didn't put Kemp behind the wheel of a car in freaked out state. Copley had never actually noticed how she'd been; he was more interested in the annoyance lying in the section. Copley's honesty was closer than they would ever be; Kemp was like them, a shadow, a mere and light impression upon the earth, soon gone.

"What you going to do now?"

The Landlord brought Copley back to the all too real world.

Copley pondered for a few seconds, answering the landlord by turning towards the little group and determinedly launched himself in their direction. He crossed. A determination of purpose that was noted with some immediate alarm by one the post grads; Copley didn't usually show such animated behaviour. How wrong she was, Copley could move with considerable speed when he either felt threatened or saw a TV crew in the area.

"Inspector, excuse me, but with your permission, I believe it would be in everyone's interest if I get the team back to work on parts of the site not inside your cordon. "

Henderson, taken aback by Copley's sudden burst of activity nodded agreement noting that everyone would be needed for further statements. Henderson had fallen into the trap of believing Copley was a pompous old fart. Pompous, yes, fart yes; but with a steely will for survival and self-promotion. Copley knew when to strike and catch opponents off guard. Copley was going to pull this one off, one dead body in the trench, one squashed into the front of a juggernaut; nothing much to worry about; these things were meat and drink to him.

Having announced his intention Copley raised his hat to the party, waved away the opportunity of another beer and swept out of the door of the pub before the temptation to spoil the act became too great.

With the main road closed and the pub phone off the hook the Press were still a little way off; giving himself an hour to get the situation back under his control Copley reached for his mobile.

Step one was to get Ernie and team back to the mess tent for a quick word re Hanna, allow for a bit of weepy emotional pat on shoulder and hugging from the spawn and then a morale boost. The show must go on, if for no better reason than Copley was teaching them to be professional archaeologists. Haha, that would be the day; valuable lessons; to be learnt, especially regarding dealing with the Press that would be landing on them. Ernie could do the warmup act and he would finish off with usual call for unity of purpose under difficult circumstances and veiled threat of potential consequences re degree grades if anyone stepped out of line.

Copley felt alive, the beer had done the trick, that and Evelyn. He couldn't afford to upset her too much.

Ernie 's gruff tones echoed in Copley's ear.
"Yes Copley. What's the plan oh great one?"

"Get the troops together in the mess tent as soon as you can
Ernie; need to give them a bit of a morale boost. Feel free to
wind them up first. I'll keep it brief. Henderson has agreed to
us carrying on. The roads still blocked, and the vultures are
still outside and I want the students prepared. We don't want
anybody speaking out of line. Make it 14:00 hours. No
absentees, three-line whip. Right, thanks for that, see you
there."

Copley redialed, this time the University and not Evelyn.
"Stephanie, can I have a word with the Vice Chancellor?
Ian, sorry to be a nuisance, but I need to keep you in touch
with developments here at Portsea. Yes, terrible business; yes,
not been dead long I would say about a week at most.
Dreadful for the students; but on the other hand, very useful
lesson in forensic archaeology; first-hand experience; can't
beat it.

Now, about Hanna Kemp; absolutely devastating for
everyone; haven't got any details yet, but haven't anything to
go on; she's, or should I say, was, a mature student, own car
and all I know is she ended up in the front of a lorry. Evelyn is
doing the family welfare bit, I'm trapped here with the
students, the roads blocked and there's only one way in and
out. Press are stuck on the outside; they can only report on the
RTA, that will get about fifteen seconds on Look North at
most.

We can turn the body in the trench to the University's
advantage; students assisted in the excavation. I was perfectly
happy to allow them to have a go; Police were more than
happy to have them on board.

I'm going to continue unless you suggest otherwise. Good. Thanks for that. See you when I get back"

Copley smiled as he strode across the pub car park. Evelyn was right, don't try and be clever, keep it straight. The Vice Chancellor had given him the support he needed. Now to make sure the students didn't give any difficulties. At the end of the day there was the Archaeology to consider and that came first, after Copley, and the students were there to prove Copley's latest theory.

Copley had dug at the coastal village of Portsea for years. Portsea, had been the Roman's major supply port at the Southern end of the Hadrianic Western Frontier; running all the way North to Bowness on Solway, where it met with Hadrian's Wall. Its main purpose was importing to troops and exporting, iron, grain, cattle, timber, wool and sheep. Where there's an opportunity there will be a trader and trade established itself early on the Cumbrian coast – long before the Romans.

Copley had recognized this fact; indeed, he had identified an earlier harbour complex than the one buried beneath Portsea Main Street. Whilst it was readily agreed that the Romans had been with Britain long before Julius Caesar provocatively disturbed the private relationships of members of the Roman Senate with their trading partners in the land of rain and mists. Copley was looking at a Roman link very far North in Britain, long established, long before Caesar.

Copley was aware that he was being followed. The two post grads were making their dutiful way back to the dig. Copley ignored them; it would be unwise to change his normal behaviour; they could think what they liked; they didn't matter. They knew the game; they towed the line or would never work in the profession; a word in the right ear could promote or destroy.

If they thought, or said he was a shit; which they undoubtedly would; well he was, but that was an easy burden to bear. He had co-operated with the Police, what other choice was there, he needed the body to be removed as quickly as possible it was in the way.

Bodies often get in the way, especially when they are in the way of new buildings. Officially burial grounds are cleared thoroughly and respectfully by archaeologists, it being a good means of income for archaeological practices. Copley remembered a case in Manchester where a priory was discovered slap bang on the site of a new development; hundreds of remains had to be removed, the project was delayed by months. The day after the site was officially cleared and the archaeologists left yet another enormous area of burials was uncovered by a JCB. That night wagon after wagon was filled with the bones and quietly tipped down the nearest mine shaft. These things happen.

Copley had no choice but report this body, far too many people saw it; he may have been tempted to work round it, had no one else been present. Why should he disturb someone else's deeds, someone else's petty little disagreements? The only difference between his skeletal finds and this body was just that the flesh; the answers were there; a mashed in face; somebody didn't want her around. There were easier methods than slaughtering people; which suggested she knew something that needed to be completely erased from history.

Copley reckoned the body would be clean this time; no immediate traces on this one. Smashing in the face was a delaying tactic; it wouldn't stop the Police; it just gave the murderer more time. The origin of the clothes, that was the biggest clue. The jaw would take time but not impossible. Delay. That was the key.

Copley mused as he crossed the field to the mess tent. He should look more closely at the section, the rest of the section, not the disturbance. Ernie had looked after general site progress and if there was anything in particular, he would have been informed; he could have missed it, if Ernie had mentioned it at two in the morning after another pint; but he was pretty certain he hadn't.

The job in hand presented itself. Portaloos like blue sentry boxes, mouldy green hues of ex-army tents and the biggest of them all, the mess tent moved into Copley's gaze. Inside; students, like insignificant pawns stood silhouetted by the canvas portal; a Greek chorus thought Copley, no farce this; a deep tragedy that needed a lift. Little groups of friends; an atmosphere of uncertainty and fear; they had been herded twice already since the find and they were ready for anything rather than another interrogation.

Copley nodded to Ernie whom was leaning back on the table facing the gathering. Copley noted Ernie's grasp of the wood, as if he was trying to squeeze the sap from it. A few more bodies made their way into the tent. A quick count and thirty-five souls stood waiting for Copley to pontificate. They would not be disappointed.

Ernie settled the throng, not that they needed much settling, a morbid silence, unusual to the mess tent, descended. Ernie read the feel well enough, he'd already had to gather the team; now he was going through the motions for his boss. He was as frightened as the rest but put up a steadfast explanation of the situation and the need to stick together, that the University would supply support.

Copley waited and as Ernie handed the floor to him, he started slowly, quietly and gently. The primary message was the show must go on; we all know what we are doing. Nobody talks to the Press without having Ernie or himself present; no going to the pub for the next two nights until the Press were out of town. The death of Hanna was tragic, and should anyone know anything else that they had not already mentioned regarding where she was going they should speak to the Police now.

What better way to celebrate a young archaeologist's life but to continue undertaking what she had set out as her life's work

Two minutes, a record for Copley, but it really was a case of showing the flag; Ernie had done the rest. Copley had sensed a complete lack of fight; they were really deflated, not by the ban from the pub; but by the circumstances. Life's work, no doubt Ms. Kemp would have gained a degree and headed for the nearest merchant bank. Get a degree in Archaeology and become something in the City.

The Police still controlled a major trench; but that wouldn't stop Copley. Indeed, it was a good excuse to consider other potentials. Copley smiled; Kemp had done something useful; perhaps a death on every dig would provide opportunity to change the plan. Copley mused on infinitive possibilities as he gazed at the sombre ranks plodding out of the tent. The really good news was the dig was to continue; there was valuable time to make up. Copley couldn't afford to have the excavation stalled, an archaeologists' reputation being only as good as the last dig. To keep spirits up, he would arrange for the students to get a delivery from the pub, the Landlord would oblige and as the students were his trade until the Press broke through the carnage, they and a few locals were his only income.

Copley happy that some order had been enforced, strode out of the tent; beckoned a passing student and asked if they could drive, with an affirmative from the unwitting soul a set of car keys were thrown at him and Copley settled himself into the Range Rover's passenger seat. The third year offered no resistance to his involuntary volunteering and duly lurched the car forward up the field and under Copley's directions navigated through the tracks up and out of Portsea. Copley had been around Portsea for over twenty years, there wasn't an inch he didn't know. There were ways out of Portsea, no tarmac and a bit on the rough side, but perfectly good ways. The Press were stuck on tarmac; the motorists would be diverted around the crash via Corey and Mireholme; lorries would be sent back for a mammoth hundred plus mile detour. The A4909 was a very bad joke, even more so than usual.

"Stop here, we will have to walk the next bit. It's Gerry isn't it?

"Jeff actually"

Copley did not reply, apologies were not part of his vocabulary.

"Let's see how bad this crash is. If we go over that fence on the other side, there is a small wood that goes through to the junction"

The pair made their way over the fence and through the wood to a myriad of flashing lights. Standing on the top of the bank looking down on the junction, or where the junction should have been the scene was truly horrific.

Five cars seemed to be fused into one; on the Buttsea bound carriageway, an HGV, it's cab facing the sky, it's wheels slewed onto the Wenport carriageway held the remains of a small blue Mazda and a Renault within it span; crushed down to a metal pulp. The trailer lay on its side with a Golf embedded in the empty space. There was blood in patches, blood on the glass, the twisted metal, there was blood, there was blood and more besides. The fire service was still attempting to remove a body from a car on the Buttsea side of the accident; an Ambulance was moving away towards Wenport, the siren breaking through the noise of unpicking carnage. In the distance there was a ribbon of cars. Stuck indefinitely. This wasn't going to be a five-minute brush and shovel job.

Copley stood utterly senseless, a mass of metal and blood. Little groups of bright yellows and greens huddled next to bits of twisted metal. This wasn't a motorway, this was just a bad junction on a bad road, a road that was a joke; a very bad one amongst a whole host that Cumbria had compiled over the years. Welcome to Cumbria where infrastructure doesn't exist because a bunch of selfish bastards didn't want the scenery spoilt. Many a time Copley had wanted the bodies of the dead delivered to the doors of the do gooders that so loved the Lake District as a simple reminder of their stupidity. The roads unable to take the traffic, the radio masts that could save lives; the idiots needed stringing up. He wished they could see this sight.

"Got your mobile Jeff?

Jeff nodded.

"Just get this recorded will you. If you can manage it from here; we don't want to interfere, just get what you can"

Jeff obliged and Copley noted he was filming the scene; such was technology thought Copley. They can build phones with video cameras, but they can't build a better bloody road. He was staring blankly at the scene, not seeing it at all, just a series of colours in his mind, Jeff could do the filming, he would see it later; he was going deeper, beyond the obvious. Copley observed the scene. He had not become a Professor for nothing; willful self-promotion only works if there is a genuine product to sell and Copley knew his skill well.

He looked carefully; there was a distinctive scorch marks on the road where a small blue car had been, save it wasn't there it was between the drivers cab of the HGV and its wheels, least what was left was. It looked for all the world as if it had been propelled there; as if an explosion had pushed it forward. He noted two suited men with vis vests kneeling by the marks.

"Jeff, get those two in suits will you, down by the junction sign"

Jeff duly turned and continued to film.

"I thought there'd just been a relatively simple head on"

"Same here; I didn't know that lass at all, bad luck on her, it's a bloody awful junction. Looks as if she just got her timing wrong and went headlong into the lorry, poor sod.

Jeff saving his efforts and putting his phone into his pocket. "Let's not overstay our welcome; I think it will be a good few hours before the road is clear"

"Day more like; must be half the Counties Police there."

Copley and Jeff made their way back through the woods to the Range Rover.

"Have you ever seen anything like that Prof.?"

"No. Never that bad, I've seen some car accidents, I've seen death many times; I've even seen a body in a trench before. No, never carnage quite like that. Sorry to put you through that."

Copley hardly ever apologized, but this was one of those moments; it was appropriate. Nobody should have to witness that; he estimated to himself how many dead, thirteen or fourteen. The scorch mark was wrong; and the Police thought so too. Should he have a word with Henderson or not; something wasn't right about that mark on the road? He couldn't say if that was Kemps car, but it was the only one actually inside the HGV cab; it was unlikely the car inside the trailer caused the accident. He would examine Jeff's efforts later.

Copley was suddenly aware that Jeff was shaking. The shock of the event was coming out.

"Come on lad, you'll be ok; a pint will soon put you right"

He broke off as the sound of a helicopter swooped over the car brushing the grass flat as it went. Only civilian markings thought Copley. The Press had landed; within a moment a second helicopter made descent directly into the field no more than 100 metres from Copley.

The only desirable factor of this intrusion was it shocked Jeff back from his stupor.

"Christ that was close"

"The Press; they'll be all over us if we don't get out of here, they obviously think we've beat them to it. Come on, get us out of here; but not to the dig they'll follow. Straight to the pub, I want a chat with Inspector Henderson"

Jeff dropped the clutch in, spinning the wheels on the mud, just as two people emerged from the helicopter; The fountain of mud didn't hit them, but it gave them a clear message. Copley looked back. Two men in suits; either the Press was dressing more smartly, or they had other reasons for being there.

As Jeff drove down the field and went to turn onto the village bound track, Copley asked him to turn left onto the Knott track. Henderson could wait. There was something about the whole scenario; especially the two men in suits at the crash site.

"You can get this through to the Castle; there's a track, bit muddy in places."

Copley was thinking on his feet. He needed to communicate with Evelyn, but for some reason he didn't feel as if mobiles were safe; that scorch mark on the road; he'd seen something of the like before. Couldn't remember exactly where, but he had. It didn't look like the result of petrol.

The Range Rover sped across the Knott and down into the woods; Jeff was enjoying himself and the car responded. Copley sat deep in thought; he didn't drive; he let others more capable do that; his mind had never got past the theory. He had tried, but his gaze would always be drawn to a feature of the landscape and that was hardly conducive of a good driver, so he had stopped. It also meant he could ponder the situation. A dead body in his trench, a dead student and dead probably because somebody had blown up her car. He'd seen the tell-tale signs in his past. That car had launched into the air. He knew what he was looking at. The men in suits; Henderson's complete lack of interest in him, simple; he knew that Copley had no interest in the students. Henderson needed a picture of Kemp's peers, not to check if she was a candidate for suicide, but because they already knew of Kemp, or at least somebody did and wanted to know where and whom she'd been with. Which also led Copley to the conclusion that an explosive device of the type used was remotely detonated for best effect. A junction being the best place; create as much carnage as possible and then the evidence of the deed can be lost in the mess. In this case somebody didn't get it quite right; the evidence was pretty clear, if Copley could see it from a distance anyone surviving the accident could do so as well. Cars don't just fly through the air by themselves from a standing start. Somebody wanted Kemp dead, and somebody must have been pretty closeby to flick the switch to get rid of her.

What Copley had to do now was get a message to Evelyn.

"Leave the car here"

They had reached the last bit of woodland before Portsea Castle. Jeff parked under the trees. Copley asked Jeff to stay put and he wouldn't be long. He was well known to the Castle, having given numerous lectures there, he'd dug in the grounds in the past without great success, but it had always been a special place for him. His first dig as a director, his first big break with the media; what heights he had reached since then.

Copley came back to reality courtesy of another helicopter passing overhead, heading for Portsea. He headed onto the lawns and into the Castle. With an uncharacteristic cheery gesture to the guides, bored through lack of tourists to herd through the rooms, he passed into the private quarters without anyone questioning him.

Copley headed for the main connecting corridor on the North side of the Castle, then turned right into the clock tower and descended into the basement. On the corridor, out of the way, was a telephone. Copley picked up the receiver, checked for a line, dialed, waited for the line to ring and then hung up. Copley did it again, and again.

Copley dialed a fourth time.

"Evelyn. I'm afraid I'm going to be tied up for a good few days here. I won't be able to make the conference in York this week. Can you cancel for me?"

Copley put the receiver down.

At the bottom of the clock tower a door led onto the terrace. Copley made his way out of the door and along the terrace; looking down along the view known as "The Gateway to Paradise"; crossing the vista, a road straddled the lowest part of the valley; strangely empty of traffic save for two heavy lifting vehicles in convoy heading towards the crash site.

"No paradise today" he said out loud.

Silence replied.

Copley strode back to the car; he reflected

Was he overreacting?

No. Copley was sure something was wrong about the whole scenario. If it hadn't been for the scorch mark on the road he wouldn't' be taking these precautions. If there was one thing anybody would tell you about Copley, other than he was a pompous drunken snob; it was you didn't take him for a fool. There was a side to Copley that only a very few knew, he kept it that way.

"Jeff keep quiet about what you've seen. Understand. You look as if you are a capable sort. This might be the making of you. You up for it?"

Jeff nodded. Noting a change in Copley. A sharper meaningful glance said it all. Copley meant it.

Jeff drove back with nearly as much enthusiasm as he had shown on the way up to the Castle. The Range Rover slid to a standby entrance to the excavation field. Beyond Copley could see the Police tape fluttering in the breeze and the tent trying to take off for the Fells. The tide had turned, and the onshore breeze would soon have it a way. Students were still working in the other trenches; their backs to the wind; huddled down into the warm depths. Copley wanted to know how things were going, but this business needed sorting first. What was going on, why kill somebody in such a sophisticated manner and whomever had done it didn't mind taking out the odd bystander in the process. Somebody wanted Kemp dead. Was it the fact she found the body?

"If the Police say anything; I asked you to take me up to the Castle as I needed to get some landscape details; as for going to the junction, we didn't go; we were reconnoitering for a series of trenches next year. I'll explain later and be prepared to go on a journey tonight, you might not be back for a day or two."

"Ok. Guess those guys in the helicopter that landed weren't from the Press then?"

"No. I think Hanna Kemps death isn't quite as straightforward as it should be and if you saw what I did, it's pretty obvious that somebody executed her and covered it up by killing a few others. You saw those marks on the road. "

"And do you think the body in the trench is related?"

"Well. As I was otherwise engaged when the body was originally found by Kemp I can't absolutely say. Did you see what happened?"

"Ernie asked me to give Kemp a hand the day before all this kicked off; she was an odd one. I mean, don't get me wrong, nothing wrong with mature students, not that she was any different than the rest of us; but she didn't mix in much. Bit of a loner; good technique in the trench, grafter, technically pretty good"

"And you'd know good?"

"Let's say, she worked ok; got the job done, recorded better than most and had an eye for detail."

"Ok, but there was still something odd?"

"Well I'm not saying that she was weird, but considering she was an HGV driver before she packed in to come to Uni. She certainly seemed to take a lot of interest in that spot up the road from here."

"Pentland Nuclear"

"Always going on about it, she'd go off on one; getting into trouble with the locals. She got banned from the pub for going on about it."

"Did you mention this to the Police?"

"The local Plod didn't take any notice really. That Henderson guy, the Detective did, but he seemed to prefer talking to the skirt, along with the sergeant. I don't think they were really interested other than that."

Copley could do nothing but agree. He'd been more worried that his neck was on the line; it was more a case of Henderson trying to get his leg over a couple of post grads. Cumbria Constabulary would be used to people being anti-nuclear, nothing out of the ordinary; especially when it came to visiting students. This was run of the mill stuff. Henderson, the sergeant and the forensic team had been in village before the Kemp 'accident'; that would be not more than hour after the finding of the body. They were locked in with the rest.

"Not a word to anyone; we're away later. As I said for several days; but be discreet. I want to make a few enquiries. Don't let anyone get to that phone of yours. Send a copy to this number. Make sure nobody finds your phone"
Copley scribbled a number onto Jeff's arm.
"Righto Prof"
.

"Less of the Prof. Copy that material send it and wash that off. Got that? Now I better prepare myself for the Press and possibly those chaps we saw up the field. Thank you, Jeff, as I say, take care and be prepared to move at a moment's notice."

Copley, needed a word with the forensic officer, Stevens was the guy in charge. Seemed a decent sort; the job done and stuck in the village there would only be one place he'd be at the time of day; the Fulford Arms. Strange the Press seemed not to have found a way from their landing site to the dig; they would. Sod the Press he could avoid them, Ernie had more than enough experience of how to handle them; he had threatened to bury a few in his time. The Police could look after the rest and if they did find him, he could bullshit for Britain as long as they were buying. They wouldn't get a thing of any note out of him. If the men in suits turned up, he would play the drunken Prof. he was good at that, it was a role he knew well.

By tramping along the headland and across the field he could reach the Fulford Arms without being noticed until he reached the pub car park; here Copley used the cut through from the Parsonage Hotel car park that brought him out for a very brief distance onto Main Street and then into the side door of the pub. Once inside Copley could breathe easy; there was Stevens with his team, a coffee in front of him and a half-eaten sandwich. No sign of the Press.

Stevens seemed relieved to see him.
"Professor Copley. Thanks again for your help. Can I get you a drink?"

A pint appeared before Stevens could move.

"Cheers"

Copley took a good swig and settled back a little on his stool to get a better look at Stevens. He seemed a pretty honest sort; bent up in the trench covered in a paper suit it had been hard to tell. Late forties and getting to old to bend much longer thought Copley; he knew the feeling, which is why he directed. Stevens seemed to be more hands on.

"Good sized team for this one; good of you to let my students in on the action. Appreciate that greatly I can tell you; nothing like in the field training. Didn't realize that Cumbria had a team like this at its disposal considering the cutbacks?"

Stevens smiled weakly. It was obvious that the greeting and pint was as far as conversation of any note was going to go.

Copley was about to enjoy fishing for information. Where had the team come from? One professional to another, all perfectly innocent; if Stevens was playing games he'd soon know.

Copley was aware that the other members of the team hadn't said a word since he'd come in. Copley recognized a stonewall and he was heading for one.

"So. You chaps are heading back to Penrith?

Silence. Deathly

Copley necked his pint and stood up.

"Can I get your team a drink?

"I'm sorry, we have to be going."

Up to the crash site?

No, another, teams dealing with that. Terrible business; we are heading out by train. Good to work with you and your students. Thanks again."

The team stood as one, collected their kit and headed out the door past Copley proffered a gesture of farewell by raising a new pint.

"Odd lot"

The barman started clearing the debris of the party's meal away.

"My brother in law's a policeman at Penrith; never heard of that Stevens feller. You were right about the Forensics; Cumbria doesn't have that many, not least at the drop of a hat; they have to borrow people from Lancashire and Northumberland. Bloody rum to me.

Have you seen the state up at the top of the hill?"

"No"

Copley lied

"Never seen anything like it, blood and guts everywhere, I counted eight cars and an HGV. That student of yours is dead and took a few more with her"

"What do you mean by 'took a few more with her?"

"Well I was out walking the dog first thing this morning when it happened, hell of a bang; would have been just about Pentland Nuclear rush hour which explains the number of cars. They come around that bend right up each other arses and the HGV came the other way and then there was this bang. Couldn't see much for the hedge but it was a hell of a bang; she must have gone straight into the HGV."

"But you didn't see it happen?

"No. That lot told me."

"But they didn't see it."

"No. But that's what they said happened, she just drove straight into the HGV.

"But they were with me; they aren't dealing with it; another team is"

"Suppose your right. Those queer ones must have heard it from the Police or their mates up at the junction."

Copley sank his second pint, the barman marked up his tab and Copley retreated the way he had come. So far so good he had avoided the Press. The rest of the village was quiet. It always was these days; the number of holiday homes had increased over the years leaving the place a ghost of its former self. Without access the village was barren of tourist hoards.

Copley wasn't imagining things, none of this horrible mess added up. He could just fall back into his happy academic world and forget all about it. Save for the fact he wasn't going to be treated like a fool. This whole business smelt. Why would Stevens and his team talk of the crash when they never went near it. Other than to get a message over. One that would be spread quickly via the pub. Where of course the Press would land any moment.

Perhaps he had brought this on himself, the Gods had decided to kick him in the goolies. It happened; some of his fellows had suddenly fallen from grace, perhaps this was his turn? No, not if he could prevent it, he wouldn't let it happen; it wasn't going to happen because Copley was going to get to the bottom of this.

Chapter Two

The Range Rover sped over the marsh as if it was floating, it was, the old coast road lay just beneath the mud, you just needed to know where it was. Get it wrong and you would be swimming soon enough. The ford across the Waynflud is a wide one and not to be crossed unless a low tide and the weather is good. Copley had decided the Southern route was the best. Whilst the main road was to be opened in the morning, Copley had other plans. The first helicopter Copley and Jeff had seen was indeed the Press. Sky News had got hold of the story and were covering both the accident and the dead body in the trench, they were even speculating a connection as the death of Hanna Kemp was duly announced to the World by Inspector Henderson. The students were kept in check by Ernie and Jeff had done as he was told, made himself ready to go at a moment's notice. Copley had done his three minutes for the news and as ever was complimented by the crew on his performance. When it came to the camera, he knew how to play it; he felt at home with a camera lens, no snotty students to look at, half asleep or drugged out of their minds. A lens was a nice safe void he could speak at and millions would see and listen.

The Range Rover splashed into the ford. Copley was more concerned about the second helicopter; that wasn't a film crew or reporters. He'd sent Jeff on a mission; the helicopter was still in the field; no sign of crew or passengers. That was at dusk. It was now dark, very dark. Copley had crept out of the Fulford Arms dressed in Ernie's coat; he suspected he was being trailed. Jeff had met him in the woods by the railway station and then headed out onto the foreshore. Copley knew every inch, whoever was following him would need night sights. Copley was guessing they hadn't.

Copley was impressed with Jeff; Ernie had given him some background information. The death of Kemp had at least made him slightly more interested in some of his students if only to make sure they wouldn't be a problem to him in the future. Jeff Blackwell; son of a farmer from Dorset; hence his expertise with the vehicle, third year student but unlikely to go further, an estate to run would see to that. Pity thought Copley. His practical skills would be better suited to working with him. Ernie needed a number two.

Safely reaching the southern bank of the Waynaflud and joining the old gun range road Copley headed South to Lancaster and then the long slog to York. No helicopter insight.

"You think there's something truly dodgy about this, don't you Prof. Otherwise I wouldn't be driving you to York in the middle of the night"

"Jeff I think you have enough intelligence to realize something is up; you don't think they were reporters in that second helicopter, and you saw the men in suits at the crash scene. It's a case of finding out what they are doing and frankly who killed both those women."

"And if whoever killed them and those at the junction, they'd kill us if they could?"

Copley already had that thought in his mind; but why would anyone want to kill an archaeology student, anti-nuclear was not a hanging offence. Plenty of people would like to kill him, that went with being an academic.

"Quite possibly. If you want out drop me off and I will make my way alone. I can't expect you to get involved."

"No way Prof. I reckon that if those bastards can have a go like that they deserve stopping. Think of the devastation they've caused to innocent people; blowing a car up like that, they deserve everything that we can throw at them"

"One thing Jeff. Stop calling me Prof., you can, and I stress only in non-academic circumstances and away from your fellow students, call me Copley. Just Copley"

The centre of York is a wonderful place at any time of day, but the hours between the last reveller staggering their way home and the first stirrings of day were Copley's favourite; when the past and the present collided; the shadows of the past and the reality merged for Copley, the shadows did not disappear for him. He had walked in the Bath house and conversed with the sentries on the gates; but that was another story.

Copley kept a flat a short distance from Queens Wharf; Evelyn was waiting for them, the coded message had worked; it was one of many and York was one of many of Copley's hidey holes, some of which Evelyn knew. Copley was convinced she knew them all, but she never let on.

Copley booked Jeff into the Queens Hotel nearby, he knew the night porter well and the name went down as Derek Watson; he was covering tracks, as he always did. Just as he had decided to travel over the Waynaflud ford; the tide would completely cover their departure; Copley could be anywhere; it would take a while for any of the traffic cameras to find the direction he was heading. Satisfied that Jeff was suitably ensconced, Copley walked the short distance to his flat.

He let himself into his flat, only to be met by Evelyn in a dressing gown and a mug of coffee in her hand.

"Morning Copley. What the hell is going on?"

"Very good question my dear Evelyn, a very good question. "You were on the news last night, only a brief moment; just enough to get the project mentioned and as an afterthought the death of one of your students and that's only because they edited the rest out. Do they know who the girl in the trench was?

They walked through to the lounge; Copley collapsed onto the sofa, weary from the journey and his mind in one of it calculating modes. Copley put his thoughts on hold, he just wanted sleep.

"Do you mind if we get to bed, I'll go through everything in a few hours; just need to rest up and get it sorted, up here"

Copley tapped his head, smiled and found himself in a deep sleep.

The sound of York going to work woke Copley up, the sunlight flooded the room. Still half-asleep Copley realized Evelyn had slipped his shoes and socks off, removed his jacket, loosened his trousers and shirt and covered him neatly with a duvet.

Copley knew full well he had a treasure, that he treated her with more respect than he did anyone else and only archaeology and possibly beer came further up his pecking order. He could smell bacon.

"Go and have a shower, breakfast won't be long; I've laid some clothes out for you. I take it you want tourist mode; don't want to be to easily recognized do we?

Copley often made his beer money taking wealthy tourists around the City. Very private tours and often sources of funding for his excavation projects would arise from these local arrangements. With at least six pubs in every walk Copley enjoyed himself as much, if more than the visitor. York was meat and drink to Copley; it was the only City where he felt truly at home. The past was ever present, and Copley could wander the streets and know that the Roman world of Eboracum lived on. The fact he had written the "worst history of York in living memory" copies of which were kept under the counter of the TIC and sold in Waterstones in the fiction section, worried him not one jot. It actually amused him; especially as he made it abundantly clear that any reader would get lost using it. That was the point. The only way to understand York was to be immersed in it. An hour in York for Copley was enough to revive him for a month. He would stand and listen to the visitors; beyond their chatter he could listen to the strands of the past. Here were his friends, alive to him, conversing happily, he would exchange gossip and past the time of day. The price of grain; the latest gossip from Rome; a party invitation and what to wear. A rabbit stew ruined by the slave and what to do about the drains at the new bath house. Copley would absorb it all. His apparent casual attitude to established fact was that most of it was complete fabrication built on speculation. His world, his understanding of the past was drilled hard to a rock of the complexities of ordinary life; reflecting little or no reality of the written record. To hell with the known, most of it was sand. The reality was there for the taking. A pile of chicken bones dumped into a road repair indicated more about the wealth of the road mender than any theory of the economic crisis during the reign of Tiberius.

Copley launched himself off the sofa and headed for the bathroom. The smell of bacon got stronger and the incentive was enough to have him fully freshened and clothed in ten minutes flat.

Sat at the breakfast table empty plate smeared with egg yoke and crumbs, Copley was prepared for questioning.

"I've got a copy of Hanna Kemps file for you; nothing much in it; just like the flat; nobody and nothing there"

Copley smiled.

"You called round to offer the departments sympathy, how proper of you, how very proper. Nothing at 127C Sandynog Lane, well what a surprise. I suppose I should be a bit surprised; you'd expect a new tenant to be there.

"The flat is being paid for, looks as if it is being used as a letter drop, the Postman still delivers, but there's no sign of a buildup of mail behind the door."

"How did you find that out?"

"There's a glass panel, you can see the carpet beyond. That and the fact I borrowed a ladder of the neighbour, told him I was looking for my cat and had a look in the kitchen window. Neat clean and absolutely no sign that anybody had been there in a while. The neighbour says a girl would go in once a week, often with a couple of men for a few hours and then come out again; always on Thursdays."

"Hanna Kemp?"

"From the description, yes."

Evelyn was used to Copley's ways; his phone call from the pub, with his "You will look into it" command gave her a clear instruction to really look into it and that afternoon she had played the part of a distressed neighbour looking for her poor Tiddles to perfection. She would have been disappointed to find a grieving partner; it would have spoilt the fun. Plus, she had an inkling that Kemp was unlikely to have a boyfriend; from the rare occasions Kemp ever poked her nose into the department office she had spent much of her time trying to chat up the young admin assistants and they were all girls. In fact, that was the only reason that Evelyn had remembered her at all. Turning up at the flat with two men seemed out of character.

Copley sipped his tea.

"I think, no I am certain that Kemp was eliminated and here's why. Copley took Jeff's phone out of his pocket, turned it on and with surprisingly little difficulty managed to find the camera menu. He handed the phone to Evelyn.

"Play the video"

Evelyn, duly pressed the screen and the scene of carnage at the junction duly began to roll. Copley waited; he knew when the most important part of the footage was recorded; he could remember the scene just as well as any digital image; he could picture it in glorious bloody technicolour.

"You see the scorched patch of road, nothing there, odd isn't it; then you see where the car is. It was where the scorched tarmac is, but it seems to have been propelled forward into the HGV. It was blown up into its path and somebody waited for the right circumstances to do it. The barman at the pub was out with his dog and saw a helicopter shortly before it happened. I bet you any money you like it was the same helicopter as Jeff and I saw land in the field near us. Why would anyone want to blow an undergraduate Archaeology student up?

"Well it's obvious she wasn't just an Archaeology student; it's not unheard of for students to live double lives; I've known a few that opened their legs and worked their way through Uni whilst their parents thought they had nice little jobs at McDonald's. I do know she was an HGV driver and she had worked in Germany during the summer; well-travelled female, unusual job. How about a drugs courier?

"Possible; certainly, would have the opportunity, the letter drop address and the men with her might fit that. But blowing her up seems a bit melodramatic; they could have easily taken her out quietly. No, they needed to bury her completely; as if they were trying to convey a message of complete accident – nothing to do with us, these things happen.

"What of the body in the trench and the students. Didn't you even consider what state they would be in?"

Evelyn was re-running the video, looking again at the carnage.

"Well you had every right to admonish me for that"
Copley thoughts went back to his first brush and trowel with death. Why had he been so calm?

"Bloody right I did. You are a complete arse when you want to be."

"I only saw Kemp when she was taken out of the trench she was in shock"

"How is the drunken bum coping with all this? Offering his unique support to all the lassies; morale boosting with his prick as ever?

"Ernie is doing a very good job; he's more resilient and caring than you think. He's keeping the show on the road."

Copley was fully aware of Evelyn's opinion of Ernie, she reminded him of it at every opportunity. He would have sulked a little, as he was often quite hurt by Evelyn's insults of his friend, but for once he would leave well alone, more pressing matters to hand.

"Thing is Evelyn, I could just forget all about this as it has nothing to do with me, the University, anything or anybody in fact. We find a body, so what; we didn't put it there. We have a student killed in a car crash – so what; nothing to do with us. But for the fact Kemp discovers the body and is then killed. Now what if somebody knew I was going to dig at Portsea; not difficult to find out, in fact all the locals know I have dug the place for twenty years plus; burying a body there isn't going to stay buried for very long. So, you say it's a complete co-incidence an outsider sees a field and decided to bury a body in it. That body went into the ground a week before I started that trench and believe me whomever buried it knew damn well, I was going to dig there."

"Because you get me to issue a site plan of the trenches for the locals"

"And when do they go up and where do they go? The murderer knew exactly where we were digging and deliberately put the body neatly into the ground right across my trench line."

"He could have done it at night, not seen the plans."

"There's a sign on the gate; why would anyone take that risk; it's not as if there aren't plenty of other places where we are not digging to dispose of a body. Why go and put it in the obvious spot. Unless you want it, found?

Somebody has decided to use me as a means of laundering their dirty washing. A disposal chute for whatever they are up to and whomever it is, doesn't mind taking out a few extras along the way"

"What do you want me to do?

Evelyn, as ever ready for the fray; Copley admired that, murder and assassins, intrigue; nothing seemed to shake her. To him it was all totally terrifying; living on his instincts came natural to him. He could cope with academic in-fighting, indeed he had plenty of tools in his arsenal. But the real thing, he needed help

Copley looked at his watch. He better call on Jeff, he'd told him to stay put.

"First things first; are all the necessary bits in place regarding my letter of sympathy, flower etcetera to Kemps family; not that she obviously has any; but as far as the University is concerned. Is the Vice Chancellor reasonably happy and can you keep him so?"

"All done; the Vice Chancellor's office believes you are doing a good job under the circumstances"

"Good job. What the bloody hell do those buggers know about a good job? Bastards"

"It's better than their usual comments about you.; now go and get Jeff round here, he might as well know about us; considering the difficulty you're getting him into."

"Are you sure; I mean nobody knows about us, it's the way you like it."

"Go on; go and get him; where you get these ideas from; the whole bloody University knows that you're sleeping with me and have been for the last twenty years. Only you keep it clandestine. Now shift and let me get on.

Copley complied. Feeling a little bruised, he left the flat and headed for the Queens. Jeff was waiting in his room, the remains of his breakfast on a tray. He'd followed instructions to the letter and not shown his face in the restaurant.

"Have you seen the news this morning; only dealt with the crash; eight dead, worst crash ever in Cumbria. Didn't name any of the victims."

Copley mused, names would be a tad difficult; allowing for families grieving, but one or two names would have normally filtered through; especially that of Kemp. Every Plod would have that on their lips; it was more and more obvious some sort of cover up.

"Jeff, I will be frank, you will have gathered that this is a very suspicious and frankly dangerous situation; I can't expect you to risk yourself; there is very good reason to believe that you could end up getting."

"Killed"

"Yes"

"These bastards took out seven completely innocent people just to kill Hanna Kemp. If you think I'm standing by to see them get away with that. Look, I can go places you never could; you'd stand out like a sore thumb; just as I can't move in your circles.

Copley knew the world he was faced with; it stung at him. Outside of his cosy, safe academia; the back stabbing the professional jealousies and squabbles; his own self-importance; he was now in his other world, a more brutal world, a world where he felt content; his blessed Roman world. A world of intrigue, courage and death; he could relate to that; he knew his territory and he knew how to play the game, he played most of it every day; his coded messages, his audience. Someone was attacking his world, attacking him; they would have to be silenced, publicly brought to book. Here was a young soldier willing to support his cause.

"Alright then, you know the risks. You might get thrown in the deep end; you will have to use your wits."

Copley eyed Jeff closely. Had he ever been like this; young, active, keen; he supposed he had; on the other hand, he had worn tweed and looked forty when he was ten, or that's how it looked now. He wasn't young, his youthful vitality had gone, gone into the soil that occupied his time; the only thing left was his ego; still as vital as ever, that and his desire for Evelyn. Here was a young man willing to do something brave or stupid; he wished he had been offered the same chance. His had been to dig, to restore a memory of yesterday and the day before that, a life in the soil and drink the juices that sprang from it.

The Newham girl came back to him. Crystal clear. A clean body save for the knife. He snapped back to the present. His start had seen tragedy, but he was part of the righting of the wrong, It, was happening again.

"I won't let you down"

"I'm sure you won't let's just hope I don't let us all down. Now come with me, there's someone you need to meet"

Back in the flat Evelyn had been busy. Inspector Henderson had left a message for Copley via the University that he could resume digging the body trench, thanking the Professor for his co-operation; other than the formalities he wouldn't be needed in the enquiry. He would be informed in due course of the identity of the deceased.

Jeff seemed less than surprised by Evelyn's presence; everyone, save for Copley, just accepted the relationship; he'd eyed her up himself; a mature good-looking woman could undoubtedly teach him a few things. Lucky old Copley; life in him yet.

"I've been making a few enquiries about Hanna Kemp. She seems to have worked for a long-distance European transport company EU Freight; based in Munich."

"How the hell did you find that out?"

"She was a mature student it's on her application for a place at the University; one of the referees worked at the same business. I rang him up, broke the news to him; seemed genuinely upset. I don't think it's the actual freight company that's involved, it's a big Europe wide concern; its more to do with the fact Hanna could drive HGV's."

"She was only 26, where did she learn to drive them?"

"In Germany, that's all I can find out, she held a German driving licence. She used it for her initial I.D on her application. We have a UK address prior to Sandynog, I'll check it out, but I can pretty well bet it will be a blank"

Evelyn turned to Jeff.

"You are off to Munich tomorrow; have you got your passport? I've officially arranged for you to be in the Orkneys for the next couple of weeks, so you have vanished. Ernie will say that you had a falling out with him and to complete your assignment you are working in the Orkneys, on North Rona. It just happens to be the remotest isle that you could possibly be on. If anybody is looking for you; they'll have to go out of their way to do so."

"I haven't, I'll need to go to my digs to get it; what about cash; I'm skint"

"I never knew a student that wasn't; buy your plane and train tickets as you go; according to my records you have A level German so you can manage. Here's five hundred pounds and two thousand Euros spend it wisely, like all students do. Ring this number on the blue phone and I will arrange for any funds; I take it you still have the same bank? Now get yourself ready. Down to the station. Off to Newcastle. Here's two mobiles. Follow the text instructions. Let me know if you think your being followed or there's a problem at your flat; though I doubt anybody would notice if it had been turned over, the state you keep it in. Be on the 07.36 to Munich from Newcastle tomorrow."

Jeff was having considerable difficulty taking Evelyn's commands in, but she fixed him with one of her looks. It all clicked into place. He'd do as she told him. This was serious. He felt a coming of age upon him. Odd. Like a curtain lifting. Evelyn was organised, suddenly he had to be. He had to come up to the mark. People were dead. Innocent people.

""What am I going for?""

"I spoke to the one person Heinrich Stumple at EU Freight he knew Hanna when she was a driver for them, he gave his home address if we needed to speak again; it would be useful if you could go and talk to him; get as much as you can on Hanna. If I'm right, it would be better to do this in person' see if you can find anybody else that knew her"

" Ok. My German isn't that good, but I'll do my best."

I will text the address and I will make sure you have some backup if need be.

Copley found it remarkable as to the enthusiasm for the task; had he ever been that enthusiastic? He watched the completely stunned Jeff. Evelyn was organised, she was the best and she knew how to keep him and his Empire safe.

"You can honestly say that you were a colleague of Hanna's, she'd mentioned him, heard the news whilst travelling and you would like to send commiserations to her family, you don't know how to contact them, See what else you can find out."

"I'll do my best"

"Whatever you can find, we've got a vacant space here; apart from attending lectures and occasionally going to her address in Sandynog nothing else, as for the boyfriend he doesn't seem to exist. At this end Copley and I will start on the body in the trench, which I think is going to be equally difficult to work out.

I've transferred your video onto my hard drive. Delete it from your phone.

If you get into trouble ring me at the University on your own mobile, just leave a message that has the word Orkney in it, I'll get back to you."

Copley wondered what he was going to have to do to match Jeff's assignment and was less than impressed to find himself at York station heading back to Cumbria. He had been looking forward to a few days in the sack with Evelyn. A man needed his creature comforts and here he was waiting for a train to take him far away from them. He stood oblivious to the world, the constant announcements the comings and the goings. He mused. Two days ago, his life had been fixed, totally secure and now it wasn't. He was still the same old Copley, the same old vindictive self-possessed pompous old fart? He was still in control?

He didn't look like himself, he stared into a waiting shelter, his reflection caught him by surprise; Evelyn had dressed him, to be precise she had undressed him, gone was the jacket, the waistcoat the bow tie, his sensible shoes. He was now anybody; chino's soft shoes, no tie, coloured check shirt; light zip up jacket and even his luggage had changed from his battered leather bag to a plastic holdall with a black zip across the top. He didn't look like Copley. He wanted to rebel; but common sense prevailed, if he was going to be treated as some kind of pawn in a very nasty game , if he was going to have to dress like the common herd, some bastard was going to have to pay for it in spades.

Copley had decided to travel to Cumbria via Manchester; a sensible move; if he was being watched he would appear to be going further away from Portsea; buying tickets on the train and paying cash would make him completely invisible; Copley knew how to be invisible; many times in his career, when things were not going quite according to his plans, he had been able to disappear without trace. His hands unsullied by the mess he had left behind. Having to dress in such clothes to do so was an all new experience that he didn't much like.

From Manchester he caught a service to Preston; he'd kept a weather eye out and was sure he was not being followed. He duly caught the last through train from Preston to Portsea.

Copley was on his way back to the dig.

"Where you been?"

The Landlord seemed genuinely concerned and not just for Copley's tab.

"Bloody place has been overrun with bloody Press. Bloody ghouls they are; asking questions of everyone. Mad business; you wouldn't believe the number of tourists we had in today, all come to see your dig. Well they came to look at the crash site mostly; a few might have gone to your dig."

Copley smiled and sank his pint; gesturing for another that he might actually enjoy the flavour of.

"You missed all the fun here, our barman's in hospital in a coma"

Copley was now listening intently.

"Found him in the field; dog sitting by him; looks as if he tripped and hit his head; poor sod. In Castletown hospital, only happened this morning, if the road had been closed, I reckon it would have been a close-run thing; as it was, they flew him to Castletown. They don't think he'll survive. Poor sod."

The occupants of the helicopter had seen the witness in the field, the man and his dog; only the man hadn't seen the actual accident. But somebody wasn't taking any chances, because the barman would talk to anybody that asked. With the road open the Press would have just sucked the place dry, so the barman had to be out of the way. A convenient fall; very convenient.

"Anything else I've missed"

"Something bloody odd about the road the day of the crash. Lads coming from and to Pentland said there were road crews out and both carriageways had those stop-go boards on them. Seems as if those poor sods were the only people on that stretch of road.

Oh, and you can tell Ernie he can let the students back in; he's kept them out of the place, the Press have gone. If one of the lasses wants a few hours behind the bar tonight I need an extra hand; it's the Young Farmers Quiz Night."

Copley acknowledged, finished his pint and made his way to the dig.

So that explained why there wasn't a queue of traffic immediately behind the accident; keeping as many witnesses away as possible. His suspicions were all too real.

He felt safe, strangely so; considering what had happened less than seventy-two hours before. Portsea always had this effect on him; it was one of those places where people looked after one another; least it had been. Times, as Copley reflected, looking at his mud-covered shoes; had moved on.

Ernie seemed pleased to see him; Copley had been right there was a significant structure where he'd said there was and the pottery was very early, earlier than anyone could have anticipated. Some good news for a change thought Copley; a world he was very safe in, that of the past.

"Everything back to normal then?"

Copley asked in more hope than anything else.

"Apart from the Press snooping all over the show; yes. Shame about the lad down the pub. These things happen. Why did Evelyn need me to cover for Jeff? You up to something, or is that a stupid question? I know you; always up to something. I can understand you wanting to cover your backside regarding the body and that Kemp girl; but frankly it's not ours, or your fault. Might look a bit odd, but we're not involved. That Jeff lad giving her one? That would be a bit odd because she doesn't go for us blokes; bloody lesbian"

"Ernie. Take it easy. You've done a bloody fine job, as ever; kept the show on the road. You know damn well I don't interfere into how you run the show and how many students you get the knickers off; that's up to you. This situation is a one off; not every day one finds a body still with flesh on it and not every day we lose a student – but more importantly not every day we have one blown up. "

"What the fuck are you going on about? Are you telling me that bloody lesbo was murdered?"

"Yes. Pure and simple and I have the evidence to prove it and I'll go as far as to say the barman down the Holly had his fall directly as a result of witnessing the crash; only the poor sod didn't witness it; others thought he had; were in a very nasty game, with some very nasty people playing it."

Copley saw that his words were sinking in. They had been through a lot, a lot of beer a lot of soil; rain, storms, droughts; students; they'd laughed themselves stupid, drunk to insanity and come up with the goods. They had lived fast and loose, won by the skin of their pants and a few knickers along the way. Copley would and did trust Ernie with his life; he had reason too; there had been some close shaves over the years. Good, dependable Ernie; sound as a pound and a bloody good archaeologist that was best when he was with students, in the trench in the pub and by his own admission his best work was always lying down, preferably on a well stacked blonde. Copley had never frightened Ernie and he was now. Ernie didn't frighten, he didn't do pale, other than in the morning after a heavy one.

"Come on Copley stop it. You can tell a good one when you want. You get things out of perspective. Yer having one of your moments."

"I wish I was. Hanna Kemp was blown up, and it was sophisticated stuff; these bastards waited till there lots of cars about to do it. To make sure the evidence got lost in the carnage. They took out eight people just to get rid of here, but the explosives must have moved, because the whole car seems to have leapt forward leaving a scorch mark on the road. You heard the helicopters'?"

"Yes. It was Sky News; they'd picked up the body in the trench story from one of the fucking students. Field day for them, spoke to the reporter; he said he was on the way back from Penrith, the Prime Minister making an announcement regarding Pentland Nuclear; got sent over here. Didn't see the second one; I thought I heard one, but frankly it was bloody bedlam here with the students all trying their best to get on the telly; poor deluded bastards. And thanks for landing me with all that shit until you got back from the village. Then you go walkabout shagging Evelyn no doubt"

Copley took it all in; he could afford to let Ernie rant, it balanced out well; Ernie did the manual bits, the looking after things, Copley did the rest. It was worth the vitriol. It was never really spiteful; it was deserved, and Copley took his medicine with a single gulp.

"What else do I do in a crisis?"

"You rely on me and Evelyn."

"Survival instinct. When I saw the mark on the road and the men in suits; plus, their friends; it was pretty obvious; that forensic team weren't straightforward either. It all began to stink, and I don't like being anywhere near a stink – it might stick. But this one could be a fatal encounter, if the barman is anything to go by."

"You're right about the forensic team; bloody good job in the trench and you didn't exactly do bad; nice to see you back in a trench, good for you, you, fat git. But; they had a way with them that made me wonder; plus, the number and they let our students in; suppose that was a plus. Not that some of them could cope. You never know how somebody will react with a stiff. But, you're right they were a queer bunch. You think they were part of what, or whoever is behind the murder?"

"I really don't know. Yes; I think so, but they were here before the road crash, before Kemps death. Did you organize where the students worked?"

"Yes, you know the score; first years on turfing, opening and barrow work. Followed by trowel technique; just to stop em digging fucking holes, and ….."

"No. I mean the second and third years; the one's that know the ropes; you know them better than me. Was Kemp any good; what was she doing in that trench?"

"Well I'd put the shoring in the day before; I was following your theory of a deep ditch cut across part of the vicus; the section was clearly showing a pretty sharp descent as you thought it would. But that sort of work is most shovel and trowel, to get down. I can't remember putting Kemp on it and with your bucket it out policy, which is as popular as sin with the students, there wouldn't be many takers; you'd have to be keen."

"You know my opinion about shoveling out of the deep, it's bloody messy and dangerous, you always end up with a pile right on top of yourself for some stupid bugger to drop back in on you. You didn't assign her to that trench?"

"No."

"Therefore, it's possible she went to that trench deliberately, because she knew there was something there?"

"It's possible, bloody odd, but it's possible. I mean why would she want to, what possible motive and when she did find the body, she was a real mess. There was no hamming it up there. She freaked. No reason for me to think other than she was scared out of her mind by the sight of a dead body."

"So we can assume that she either expected, or hoped not to find anything; and if she did, that's what caused her to freak out; which means she had prior knowledge of something going on and it being right in the middle of my excavation." "Thus, the body was deliberately put there to be found?"

"Exactly. But why didn't you notice the ground disturbance when you de-turfed it should have stuck out like a sore thumb?"

"There you have me. I left it to a group of first years to dig it out; I was pushed for bodies. There's a good surface we know at one end and I just told them to follow it down as it began to submerge. Had a third year check the finds; usual piles of pot, some nondescript metalwork. I was too busy, frankly there was more pressing work."

Copley couldn't complain; if he had spent more time on the dig and less time in the pub perhaps this wouldn't have happened? No. It was planned to happen; somebody was playing games and Copley didn't like it. He relied on Ernie too much; he would mend his ways; but he wouldn't, he at least would think about it and that counted, as far as Copley was concerned; conscious clear.

"I only saw the grave cutting marks when I was helping the forensic team. Tall chap dug it and pretty damn healthy, the cut was sharp, the spade marks suggested power and fitness. Suppose I should have said something at the time; but I just got stuck in. You know I really enjoyed it? I really did. I suppose they knew I would. 'let the old bugger have a play with the stiff, keep him busy. Let some of his students have a go -what a lark, see how they throw up after seeing the face.' Bastards, fucking bastards."
"It wasn't a sledgehammer"

"What?"

"It wasn't a sledgehammer."

"Well what was it then?

"The impact wound would be a lot bigger; the maxilla was utterly caved in I'll grant you but the frontal had the skin rolled back; if that had been a sledge it would have crushed it in. Wasn't a sledge and to get that blow the way it hit she was unconscious or dead when it was inflicted; too precise, she would have struggled if she was awake. It's disfiguring to slow down identification."

"I agree with that."

"The forensic bod, Stevens; he agreed with me when he was tidying up; the knife seemed to be the obvious cause of death, the rest was just to put a bit of distance between the doer and the done. You know that she wasn't exactly well dressed under that mac; like the fanny that totters wear down Northumberland Street on a Saturday night; not the sort of gear you wear in West Cumbria."

"That would explain the shoes"

Ernie smiled; knowing Copley's delectation.

"Too right. Not what you wear in a field in Cumbria."

"Have you seen Henderson?"

"No, just the sergeant sniffing around a post grad the dirty bugger; he won't get far. No interest in this murder whatsoever; as if it had never happened. Now if this was the middle of Manchester, I could have sort of understood it, but this is rural Cumbria; people don't just end up dead on a daily basis. The locals think it's odd; talk of the pub last night, but it got relegated to the bloody business of the accident at the junction and who gets the bar job at the Holly now the Barman's gaga. The County Council were up at the junction re-surfacing the road; according to the locals, they've never moved so quick.

What a surprise thought Copley. The road re-surfaced, all the evidence of the scorch marks removed. Normally the Police would have the place treated as a crime scene for ages; the traffic accident guys would be out measuring and re measuring every inch. And yet it was all buried under new tarmac. Copley's mind turned to the suited men at the scene; no doubt they had ordered the road to be covered as soon as possible; just as they had silenced the barman; because Stevens had told them he was shouting his mouth off. Was he going to be next? No. It was if the whole thing was set up to make sure the body was found; found by somebody that the establishment trusted – more fool them.

Ernie 's mobile rang.

"Hello Gorgeous"

It was Evelyn. Copley knew Ernie s greeting well enough. Evelyn tolerated Ernie, but always at arms-length; mostly because of her desire to kick the shit out of him and had from time to time done so; but her anger did sometimes get the better of her. Staff Christmas parties were a minefield; Copley quite enjoyed them; he would wander through them in a haze of fine champagne. The last department to have a proper wine budget, that was Copley's boast; it was a simple toss-up between an extra member of staff, or the wine; the wine always won.

"Right I'll tell him. See you darling."

Copley grimaced; he heard the sharp 'fuck off' before the line went dead.

"I'm to tell you that your paperwork for Germany is safely on its way and the Vice Chancellor has issued a statement regarding the continuation of the excavation and the fact we assisted the constabulary. "

"Well it's nice to see our Vice Chancellor so on the ball; no mention regarding a statement on the death of Hanna Kemp?"

"No."

"I take it you were your normal diplomatic self with Kemp. I mean you will have tried it on and as you've suggested she resisted your designs? You've suggested she was batting for the other side; but if that is the case that would be nine tenths of the entire female population of the globe; what did you really think of her?"

"She was good in the trench; went on a lot about Pentland Nuclear up the road; there was something not quite right about her and I don't mean her turning me down; they all do that, well until they've had a few. She kept herself pretty much to herself. I've talked to all the second years and they no more than they've told the Police. The strange bit is the HGV driving; why give that up to go digging with shit pay and prospects?"

"It is a vocation, a calling."

"Bollocks"

"It hasn't done you any harm."

Copley and Ernie would have launched into a grand row that undoubtedly would have concluded at four the following morning with one or both falling off bar stools in the Fulford Arms. But it was not to be. The sergeant wandered into view still in deep conversation with the post grad from the Fulford Arms of two days ago. Copley instinctively smelt trouble.

"Professor Copley, might I have a word."

The sergeant seemed relaxed enough. Copley anticipated a little play acting on the sergeant's part; he was out to impress his new girlfriend; putting the old fart in his place would assist in his sordid little cause; no doubt the uniform was the turn on. As far as Copley could tell there was precious little intelligence to spark any other interest between the two of them. Overture and open the curtains; act one, thought Copley.

Miss Preston has been very helpful in our enquiries and I wonder if you wouldn't mind explaining the reasoning behind the excavation undertaken in the trench where the body of the young woman was found?

"Well sergeant I'm very pleased to see that our students are continuing in helping with your enquiries; least we can do under the circumstances. Miss Preston is a post-graduate; no doubt she will have you informed you that I have undertaken excavations in and around the Roman settlement of Portsea for the past twenty years. This particular site is the earliest Roman site; the first point of contact between the natives and the Roman traders. If you mean to ask why I ordered the excavation where I did it was the result of work undertaken some years ago. Resistivity surveys and magnetic resonance in this case; all fully documented. If you mean why I went straight in; rather than take a more cautious method, I was aware of the occupation layer, which we have found elsewhere previously and the sharp decline into the ditch; not all trenches need to be precise, nor do they require my personal attention"

"Why did you instruct Hanna Kemp to be moved from her work elsewhere on the site to work in this trench?"

"Very simply. I didn't. The day to day working, the supervision of the site is in Ernie 's hands. He makes these decisions as he sees fit to the activity in hand."

All the party looked at Ernie; whom somewhat surprised by the turn in the conversation, simply responded.

"I didn't"
"You gave no specific instruction for Hanna Kemp to work in that trench?"

"No, definitely not; she volunteered to work it; I've mentioned this before. She specifically offered to work it"

''She told me you'd ordered her to work it; she was pretty 'narked' as she was busy with a section of hearth; she was collecting charcoal samples and you had ordered her back to a pick and shovel job as she saw it.'''

Miss Preston was digging the trowel deep into Ernie. Fortunately for Ernie he was more than capable of deflecting the attack.

"Kemp wasn't doing any hearth work; she was in the exploratory trench down by the river; I wouldn't have called anyone back to the body trench; Kemp had volunteered. Anyway, I've already mentioned this yesterday. What's new in this?"

Ernie was indignant and glared at Preston with a look suggesting her career archaeology was in the balance; with boot about to weigh it downwards.

The sergeant, realizing he was about to be left behind in a developing academic spat went for the jugular; his chance of repeating his leg over of last night never being repeated was likewise as uncertain as Preston's future. He didn't get the chance.

Copley was the first to hear it and swung round.

A helicopter was making its way past the Knott; low and fast; then still and descending. Copley froze; it was the same helicopter, the men in suits. Were they all in danger; Copley's mind went into panic mode? Where was Evelyn when you needed her; was this it; the end. Should he run, should they all run?

The door of the helicopter opened; two suits emerged ducking down below the slowing blades.

This was it. Death was staring at Copley. The suits approached. Copley looked to the hands. No guns; that was a start, it was looking a little brighter, but what of the pockets?

The suits approached and Copley eyed the two men, not quite as young and fit as he had anticipated; if he was going to die, it was the by the hand of two mid- thirties accountants with ill-fitting suits. Grey haired and balding, bespectacled the only difference was about six inches in height in his favour.

Suit one approached; the little group had gone very quiet; Copley expected the worse. He loved Evelyn, he wanted to see her again, he would do anything to see her; he wouldn't beg, he would fight; he would fight to stay alive. Here were the two men that he'd seen at the crash scene; part of whatever team Stevens belonged to. Part of a cover up and lethal; there was a barman in a coma courtesy of these two.

"Professor Copley"

Suit One broke the silence.

Copley stepped forward. He was sweating now, he was angry; angrier than he had ever been, he was seething inside; fear turned to anger; his head ached he was breathing deep, deep and fast.

Copley's step turned into a half gallop and rugby tackle, launching himself at Suit One; yelling to Ernie to get Suit two. Copley's action took all by utter surprise; but Ernie instinctively followed Copley's lead and had Suit Two on the deck with Ernie following through with a kick to the groin.

Ernie seeing Copley's intended boot to the head on Suit One was a step too far held him back.

"Yer don't have to kill him, he's not going to put up a fight; nor's the other one; he's out cold. If you don't mind me asking Copley, what's the fuck going on? You certainly didn't give me a warning this was going to turn into a punch up; who are they?"

"These chaps were at the crash site, looking at the scorch sites; there's more; two came after us when we came back from the site. Have a look in his pockets will you, I feel a bit sick."

Copley stood up; he felt exhausted, he leant on his hips, slowly standing to his full height; he looked at the sergeant and Preston. Neither of which had moved, frozen for a moment. He turned towards the helicopter; another person was getting out; another suit. The sergeant broke free of his stupor; Preston turned and ran up the field; the sergeant instinctively ran after her; escape, or an excuse for an escape thought Copley. It wasn't over yet, but at least they knew Copley wasn't going down quietly and now Ernie was on the case the picture looked a little rosier. He gasped; the rugby tackle had rattled him, but not as much as it had the suits, they were out cold.

"Ah; this could be a bit awkward. You do pick them. I think we may have some questions to answer"

Ernie was taking in the opposition and their situation and it wasn't looking good.

"Why?"

"Let's put it this way; he's seen us try and rugby tackle and I haven't much puff left"

Bring it on. Thought Copley. He'd never felt like this. Evelyn; she should be here, even if he went down in a hail of bullets, he would have stood up by himself and given it his best. With Ernie by his side he felt invincible.

"Professor Copley?"

Suit three looked younger, fitter; not such a push over as the other Suits; this might take more doing; but bring it on.

"Professor Copley"

"Who wants to know?"

"Donald Fremlins, MI6"

"Ah."

Copley looked at Ernie ; Ernie took the Suits pass at arms-length. Copley didn't look at it too closely. His head was swimming. He felt sick again, a deep gut-wrenching feeling;

"I see you've met Gregg and Biggs. Not bad professor; we didn't have you down as being able to look after yourself so well"

Fremlins looked genuinely impressed with Copley; which brought him back to his senses; Copley wasn't being shot at, nor was he being forcibly restrained at gunpoint. All was looking much brighter. It looked as if he had just hit the good guys, but how was he to know it; they weren't exactly obvious.

"You certainly put the fear of God up those two; the sergeant seems more frightened than Miss Preston. Don't worry we'll catch up with them. Now if you don't mind, we'll get these two back into the land of the living."

Fremlins wafted a small phial of smelling salts under the noses of the two prostrate officers; the results were positive; The Suits sprawled about on the ground getting their senses back; hearing Fremlins voice prevented any retaliation. They sat on the grass head between the knees in abject misery. A fat old professor and his side kick twice their age had flawed them; it didn't look good for their reputation. Hurt pride hurt more than the cracked ribs that Copley and Ernie had inflicted. Copley felt not a moment's pity or regret; he had been fighting for his life; there were no rules – he knew that from a life in academia.

"Now professor; I have an apology to make. I made the decision not to involve you in this matter. My call, and it was a bad one. I fear that we have to involve you in a particularly delicate situation; I think under the circumstances you and Mr. Tricker better join me in the helicopter.

Greggs; you and your partner pick the sergeant and Miss Preston up; I'll radio for a car. Take them to HQ. Now professor if you don't mind."

"I've a site to run"

Ernie ever the practical, undeterred by flattening an MI6 officer or two had, as per his norm, archaeology on his mind.

"I'm sure the students can manage for a couple of hours Mr. Tricker; I assure you; you will be back safe and sound before closing time."

Copley mused that Fremlins knew all about them; every sordid detail of his life; at least he could relax; he wasn't going to be shot or arrested and the University couldn't say a word; he was co-operating with the authorities. He would see Evelyn again. He was alive, he was Copley again.

The three made their way to the helicopter and with very little ado and before Copley had fully understood the workings of his seat belt, were airborne flying along the coast and then inland around the perimeter of Pentland Nuclear; across Whitehaven and right towards Cockermouth; land that Copley knew well. They were following the river Derwent and swung down to the unmistakable pink tower of Isel Hall.

Copley had spent many happy hours at Isel; the magnificent and ancient pile, as old as time. The helicopter landed on the lawn and after Copley was extracted from the tangle of his seatbelt, he found himself enjoying the rambling frontage of Isel. A rotund well-suited grey-haired creature was smiling at them from the terrace steps.

Ernie was calmly led away towards the west wing by Fremlins, with the offer of refreshment. Copley knew it was never difficult to gain Ernie's attention. Whilst Ernie went West, Copley was beckoned to the East.

Copley felt safe and tired. It must have shown.

"Professor Copley, my dear sir you look exhausted; come, sit. I fear we have put you through considerable perils in the last couple of days. Sit yourself down. Tea. No, I anticipate something in the way of an Ale would be more to your liking"

Copley knew this gentleman well, at least professionally, He'd seen him only a couple of months before; at Burlington House. Sir Seymour Thwaites; Society of Antiquarians; a fellow ancient historian with some notable papers to his name, in particular a paper on the re-interpretation of findings regarding the green sand forts of Surrey. A project that Copley remembered had been close to his father's heart, he'd worked them with Sir Mortimer Wheeler. Thwaites had re-examined the work and suggested the forts had been occupied; rather than the view held by Wheeler that they were only for defensive purposes. A view that Copley agreed with; he'd seen the inhabitants.

A young Copley had spent a day at the fort by himself; a mistake in the digging diary had found him stranded at the site. It was a wonderful sunny day; the best of summer weather; the cool of the shade, the glisten of golden light all made for an illuminated adventure. Copley had explored the fort ditch and entrance gateway to his heart content, the excavations were well advanced, the detail of construction was laid bare. After a couple of hours Copley had become increasingly aware that he was not alone. It was less a feeling, more a reality; he was surrounded by activity; by people; by buildings, by cattle. The sensation was so strong; then as slowly as it had come upon him it suddenly went; the fear only came once it had passed. So frightened he ran down the hill to the pub. But as he ran it felt as if he was missing something, he was running away from the past and the past dragged him back. He re-climbed the hill, step by step knowing what he would find. The sun shone, the place was a summers grove and then, just as before, there were the buildings and the people; he could smell the hearths and cattle he could hear the past and he sat and stared at it, listening to a tongue he couldn't understand and then he realized that they could see him. This wasn't a one-way experience; they could see him.

Copley had fled. His Father realizing the mistake regarding the day had headed out to pick him up and found a white shaking Copley waiting by the pub at the bottom of the hill. But had his Father forgotten, perhaps he knew more than he let on, perhaps he realized that Copley had inherited some ability to see the past; to be part of it and that could only be, if he had the skill himself? Copley would never be sure; a test; not beyond his Father. Perhaps the fear had made him more aware, shaken the connections in his minds, opened up new pathways into the past?

Copley knew that Thwaites had a good eye for the past; pompous prat he maybe; but solid in archaeology. He could trust him, to a degree; archaeologists, good ones, instinctively know to look beyond and Thwaites was obviously employed to do just that, whatever the problem. As Copley had often said; 'never mess with an archaeologist.'.

"Seymour Thwaites; green sand forts; excellent work, I heartily agree with your findings. I find you in unexpected company"

Copley nodded toward the helicopter out on the lawn.

"Thank you, Copley, I may call you Copley; I believe everyone does?"

Copley smiled.

"As you know everything about me there's absolutely no reason why you should not. If you expect me to apologize for hitting your two officers I will not. If you had come clean as to what you were up to it would have been different story. I expect I'm not in a position to ask what the hell is going on, but I will anyway?

Thwaites had raised his arm and a steward, some way off, strode across with a couple of bottles of beer, glasses and sandwiches.

"MI6 are the foot soldiers in this matter; all I can say at this stage is Her Majesty's Government requires your assistance in a very delicate matter. Basically, our adversaries left a calling card and you picked it up."

"The body in the trench"

"Precisely."

"Why me?"

A good question. But first I should reveal that all is not as it seems.

"Hanna Kemp, your mature archaeology student; though it amazes me a twenty-six-year-old can be called mature; has an interesting background. Namely she isn't Hanna Kemp. In fact, she is Erika Schneider, a member of a far right neo Nazi group based in Bavaria; headquarters in Munich. It appears she acted as a courier; her HGV licence allowed her easy access to all parts of Europe; working as a contract driver.

The real Hanna Kemp was the body in your trench. Not at the junction.

Copley stared into the distance taking this revelation in. Suddenly not having anything to do with his students made sense. He inwardly relaxed, thinking to himself how the university would take the news. They wouldn't of course Thwaites and his friends would make sure of that.

Kemp was a hooker, Schneider stole her identity when she worked in the Lieerkasten in Munich. They must have done their homework, they picked a girl that was remarkably similar in all respects to Schneider, didn't even need to dye her hair; same build, height., everything as an HGV driver she could spend time researching girls to find the right match. Kemp befriended her, got her to leave the very profitable establishment she was ensconced in; set her up in a flat and effectively kept her as her lover and by doing so had access to her passport. Thus, Schneider passed to and fro, enrolling as a student at Castletown and living in the student life. She chose archaeology at Castletown because of your work; the key factor being it was long term and close to Pentland Nuclear."

"What was she actually doing. I can see the subterfuge?"

Copley sank his beer and waved at the steward who responded.

"Well she was certainly trying to subvert your students. Miss Preston in particular; she'd suggested that Preston could oust your supervisor by suggesting there were grounds for a sexual harassment allegation; she also was openly anti-nuclear"

"Yes, I'd heard she was banned from the pub for just that."

"Bit of a smoke screen the 'anti-nuke' bit I think; nothing unusual that, but getting rid of the experienced dig supervisor in a way that you couldn't defend because everyone knows his track record and he would have to go even if the allegation was unproven, there might be some mileage in that."

"What possible benefit would there be in that?"

"Because with him out of the way an influx of students from outside would be possible; your chap may have his, let us say, idiosyncratic way, but he is very efficient and knows the job and his students inside out.

"Especially the women."

"Without him a couple of new faces wouldn't be noticed. Let's be perfectly honest Copley you maybe the country's leading Archaeologist but you wouldn't have the faintest idea about those that do the work for you."

Copley ignored the slur on his character; there was no point denying it, he had no idea about his students. More precisely he didn't care and this experience was not exactly improving his humour or consideration of them any more likely.

"To what end? To what end could she possibly be able to do anything? , I mean even if she had a few extra hands on the job for some nefarious purpose she could hardly of done any damage at Pentland Nuclear, it's pretty well protected from what I can see. The chaps on the gate wander about with some pretty big pop guns. You don't expect me to believe they were going to attack the place?

Now what I cannot fathom is why would Schneider want to dig Kemp up; getting Ernie out of the way would be useful for that, but the point is there are eight different trenches on the site and how come she knew exactly which one to dig in?"

"Kemp had a trace device on her. It was still transmitting; Kemp just had to follow the signal."

"She wasn't wearing much"

"It was in her belly button ring."

"Schneider kept a very close eye on Kemp then?"
"Not close enough. Not even her Neo Nazi colleagues knew she had left Munich; we picked her up on our monitoring equipment two weeks ago. She travelled by ferry to Castletown, called at Sandynog Road then caught the train to Carlisle, then down the coast to Portsea."

"What then?"

"She met with your friend, the barman at the Fulford Arms. We have him custody; it appears he unwittingly acted as a go between. We need him out of the way, at the moment, besides, as Kemp and Schneider were eliminated it seems likely he would be next"

"And the eight poor devils at the junction"

"Precisely"

"Why if Kemp was apparently so happy in Munich did she make a bolt for it and why come to Portsea?"

"She knew, or thought she knew that she'd be safe; small out of the way place like Portsea; she could wait for your team to turn up, Schneider wasn't at Sandynog when Kemp called; she obviously thought Kemp was already at Portsea."

"Why didn't she just ring her?"

"Whatever the message was, it wasn't for transmission, suggesting Kemp was bringing a message from a third party. She went to the flat, expecting to see Schneider, but she wasn't there, she doesn't seem to have waited around; we think there was somebody with her that stage, some bodyguard or possible assailant."

Copley mused; if Evelyn's chat with the neighbour was right it had been Kemp with two men; he was ahead of the game and would keep the information to himself. He wondered if Jeff had reached Munich or had Seymour had him intercepted? Copley would have to hope not. If the Holly's barman could disappear it could be an equally rough time for Jeff.

"So, Kemp turns up in Portsea a week before we arrive; gets killed and buried in my trench, very precisely; in my trench. Perhaps I should say deliberately planted in my trench"

"I would agree; a warning to Schneider and her friends. We know she made a call to Munich shortly after the body was found; to one of her work colleagues at Inter Europe.

Your intentions were very clear, anyone could have followed the plans and popped the body in just waiting for you to dig her up. Bit embarrassing for you that nobody noticed the disturbed soil."

Seymour half smiled as he sipped his beer. Copley was cornered, he couldn't avoid the fact he hadn't noticed the turf being disturbed, nor had he been aware until the body had appeared that anything unusual was happening in that trench. True, he had gone at it hard, he had given Ernie instructions to get down into the ditch and to find it within the first couple of days and he was cutting corners to do it, but a grave like disturbance would have shown up like a sore thumb if he'd seen it and he hadn't because he was in the pub. First years digging holes; he'd left it to first years, or to be precise he had left it to Ernie, to first years and that was likely to get the quick depth he needed and sod the archaeology along the way. Copley drank deep. He was in the skip with this one.

"I wouldn't be too hard on yourself; you did have, how many trenches open in the first week?"

"Eight. Some were mere sondages, but I should have supervised the trench better."

"Even so; you had an enormous task to tackle, you couldn't be everywhere. I shouldn't worry about it. We all have our little problems and anyway nobody will much bother about Kemps body; it will be reported to have been in the ground for years. Kemp will vanish from history, as far as we are concerned, she moved to Germany and was never seen of again. "

Copley wondered what was going on; why was he being exonerated by Seymour Thwaite?

"You won't see anything in the Press regarding the Kemp body; D notice, as for your students and those that worked on the body, well, let us say, they will never say another word on the subject. All will have signed the Secrets Act of their own free will by now and their student fees will be sorted out in time. As for the village, we will make sure the body found turns out to be Roman; lying in the ground for the last eighteen hundred years. All tidied up for you.

We will be bringing Miss Preston in for questioning, we believe Schneider may well have told her something of what was going on; she'll co-operate, not to fear; they always do. As for her new policeman friend he will be sent a long way away.

We can't have your supervisor put to any trouble over allegations of sexual harassment can we; you have a very good archaeologist there Copley. But you know that, don't you; the best team we could have and for once its batting for us"

Copley was not in the slightest worried about Miss Preston; in fact, he could quite happily have turned the thumbscrews himself. He was relieved that his reputation was intact; but annoyed that it was a case of a favour to be returned. As for Ernie; well he would be grateful for another pint; and that would do.

"And in exchange?

Seymour, your bounty comes, no doubt, at a price; which of course I will accept; because I have just been flown here to drink your beer and been set free from one all mighty heap of shit?"

"All in good time Copley. Have another beer."

The steward appeared with another two bottles and a fresh tray of sandwiches. The sun shone on the silver tray; the stone of Isel Hall seemed to be gently roasting in the sunshine. Below the Derwent washed past the great cliff holding the Hall aloft. A Hall had stood here long before the Normans, a boundary marker, facing South, dominating the scene, for a long-forgotten age when Britannia had fallen into chaos and loss. The scent from the borders wafted through the walled garden and away on the breeze. On such an afternoon could such skullduggery be afoot thought Copley, indeed it was and he was ready to listen to the tale.

 "We have reason to believe that Kemp was carrying something with her when she was killed."

"Do tell."

Copley was beginning to enjoy himself.

For a starter the location was a lot more comfortable than Copley had expected, Some hi-tech underground bunker deep under Manchester, or Glasgow. What Seymour Thwaites was doing at Isel, was, like everything else, more than somewhat puzzling. Copley was enjoying a beer and a sandwich, making the most of the sunshine and the view and Seymour was obviously not as clued up as he had expected, there were chinks of light showing through. Copley hoped Jeff was on the case. He could rely upon the lad; Evelyn seemed confident enough' or she would have stopped him from going.

"We believe she was carrying a highly sophisticated detonator mechanism."

"For a bomb?"

"Precisely. For a bomb."

"Wouldn't our border security gubbins stop her from entering fortress Britain? Why didn't you pick Kemp up; if Schnieder was pretending to be Kemp she would have had to have her passport; so how did Kemp get in.?"

Schneider could move around Europe on her own passport; she only needed to be Kemp as an additional identity; for University, for Council Tax; she even took an HGV test in Kemps name."

"Weren't you watching her?"

"Yes, but we were only interested in her neo Nazi activities; all relatively low key; no reason to remove her."

"Then it all turned nasty"

Copley could tell Seymour was uneasy; it was becoming obvious that Seymour was trying to manage a situation out of his hands; somebody was playing catch up. No wonder it was a case of keeping radio silence and offering olive branches. Copley brought Seymour back to his question.

"This bomb: are we talking some sort of nuclear device?"

"We don't know. What we do know is that any nuclear material brought close to any of our nuclear sites would be identified by the monitoring equipment."

"Kemp walks into the country with a nuclear detonator in her handbag, which we both know we haven't found yet."

"She wasn't carrying any nuclear material in; the detonator could be in a series of parts; but we do believe she carried it in and that she was intercepted."

"Well she certainly didn't take the front of her face off by herself. So you have no idea where the detonator is, what it looks like, a trail of dead bodies, most of which are poor fucking innocent bystanders trying to enjoy the Cumbrian scenery and no doubt no idea of where and when and whom are going to attack us, if it's the UK that is going to be attacked. Sounds a good one Seymour"

"Which is why we need your expertise"

"I'm an Archaeologist; I know that we have a fearsome reputation, but we don't normally mess in the nuclear world, nor espionage for that matter. We like nice quiet lives stabbing each other in the back and getting pissed at conferences. So how can I help, as I owe you one for keeping me out of the poo; even if the poo is of your making for letting this Schneider woman loose? By the way who killed her; not your lot then?"

Seymour stayed silent.

"What is it you want me to do?"

"We want you to carry on working at Portsea."

"I was; before all this all kicked off"

 "Whomever is behind this is playing a game; we don't think it's Schneider's group; her neo Nazi's network; why would they have any great interest in such a show? If they wanted to attack a nuclear facility, they could hit anyone they like in Germany. Somebody knew of their network infiltrated it and used it to their own ends. Burying the body on your patch was part of a message. "

"Is that it? Come on Seymour, I know you better than that, you always were devious; I've always wondered about the Society Antiquarians and you've done nothing to make me think otherwise. Come on out with it?

Copley was feeling much more confident and even more suspicious. Seymour was relying upon his MI6 colleagues and it was obvious they were not coming up with the goods.

"We expect another message. Kemps body; the detonator; Schneider blown up; there's more. Why they are going to these lengths is beyond any of us; if you were going to commit a major act you'd just get on and do it. It's as if we are meant to be the audience for a performance, save we don't know where the show is."

"Mugs more like. Seymour wouldn't whoever is behind all this is be miles away; they will know you've been all over the shop.

"That undoubtedly is true. But we couldn't do anything else; we have to go with along with it; Pentland Nuclear is the nearest and most obvious target. Cumbria doesn't have anything else that would attract international attention"

"They could be planning to blow up Peter Rabbit. They'd have my support for that one. So. Seymour you want me to go back and let my students be targets; I have to say that much against my opinion of students, that even I think that's a bit harsh on them. "

"Your secretary Evelyn; she has been very helpful."

Copley remained outwardly relaxed: the beer assisted; he had expected Evelyn's name to appear. It was true they were the worst kept secret; but what did Seymour know; not a lot it seemed; other than academic tittle tattle. He looked down the lawn, into a personal distance, beyond the trees, deep into his self. There was something about Isel that Seymour had no idea of; its tunnels. Beneath the hall, beneath the walled garden, beneath the lawns and down into the secret grotto. Constructed to frighten and delight; mysterious, alarming and all man made; all illusions. Illusions that Copley knew were meant to divert the viewers' attention from the facts. Isel held its secrets well; Copley knew.

"Copley. Are you with us?"

"Yes, sorry Seymour; just thinking. Go on."

"Evelyn; she has been very helpful. Without her we couldn't have acted so quickly regarding your students. You're very lucky."

"I know"

Copley surprised himself. He never admitted to Evelyn's abilities; it would reveal his inadequacies; he was slipping. His pomposity was cracking; he feared it would; she had begun consuming him years ago, she nearly had. Truth being he loved her; he hated to admit it, he loathed all that went with partnership, he hated taking anyone else into his inner thoughts. She was there, she invaded his being and he enjoyed it, oh how he enjoyed it. The arguments, the rows the verbal abuse; the lightness of her touch; her skin; her legs, oh those legs.

"Copley"

"Ok Seymour; of course, I will carry on as normal."

"I assure you; we will not let any harm come to any of you"

"That's reassuring considering what's happened so far – let me see eight innocent people dead and one being held for his own safety. That makes me feel so much happier. We'll be the decoys in the pond"

"We will have some officers working alongside your students and there will be more about that you won't see."

"I bet we will. You can't do anything in Portsea without somebody knowing about it"

"You mustn't underestimate us you know; we got the barman out in one piece"

"You still have eight grieving families; not exactly a draw is it. If that's a triumph, I hate to see what else you can manage; well I suppose I know, don't I?

Copley was beginning to feel belligerent; Seymour had the power to destroy his career, even make him disappear; but he too was vulnerable. For all his technology, he was as much in the dark as anyone else.

Seymour stood up.

"Well I must be off; good to see you Copley. As I say just carry on as normal; your new students will fit in very nicely; their fully briefed and Ernie will be busy getting to know them now; he's in the dining room with them; one or two of them took archaeology at University, so I don't think he will be to upset at the prospect. We will just wait for developments; see what happens."

"Well that puts me completely at ease doesn't it. I take it I don't have to keep in contact; your people do that"

"Precisely. All you have to do is dig as normal and I look forward to your findings. Don't worry about anything else, everything has been duly tidied up; just enjoy yourself. Now you must excuse me. The helicopter will take you back when Ernie has been fully introduced to our team. Relax, enjoy yourself; wonderful place Isel, I simply must come here more often."

Seymour strode away towards the Hall, leaving Copley sitting in the afternoon sun. It was an opportunity to ruminate; another beer would help , the steward could save himself sometime by bringing four bottles to keep him going.

Copley considered how the land lay; his career was in Seymour's hands; Seymour could still squash him if he liked, even if he co-operated. Copley had long learnt the treachery of academia; it would be no different in the land of spooks. He needed to do his best to protect himself; Evelyn was the key to that and Jeff; Jeff, if he could get information and not have anybody pick him up; well, that could be very useful. Could he manage it? More to the point if the other students had told Seymour's men that Jeff had vanished that could be more than a little difficult. Seymour undoubtedly underestimated students; Copley didn't take any notice of them, but he did know they could be stubborn and close ranks; they could be petulant. Gone were the days of anti-establishment; student loans and anxious parents had done for that. They were more compliant; more demanding and more cunning. They would undoubtedly fall for the bait of tuition fees in return for silence. But that silence might just include where Jeff was. But he was hoping for too much, somebody would drop him in it. The cover story might hold; Ernie had spelt it out; but he might still need to produce Jeff like a rabbit out of the hat. He needed Evelyn.

Ernie emerged through the dining room French windows. He ambled across the lawn.
"Well that's a turn up for the books. I was expecting the third degree."

Ernie sat himself down and helped himself to a beer. The steward was beckoned over and further replenishment of stocks for the journey back were duly organised.

"We have Seymour's helicopter to take us back, very nice."

"And his officer working with you and goodness knows what and whom all around us. And we're supposed to carry on as normal. Some hope of that."

"It could be worse. I take it your reputation is intact."

"As is yours."

"All we have to do, is sit tight and carry on."

"Do you honestly believe Seymour won't drop us in the shit once this is all over?"

"No. I think you will be dropped in it from a dizzy height. Word to the right people and you will be history. As for me, God knows what he could do to me. But there is a good side to it."

"Do tell"

"It gives us time to dig ourselves out and get something on Seymour"

"I suppose it does. You ready; we better do as we are told, the pilot looks as if he wants to leave"

The pair wandered over to the helicopter.

Looking down on west Cumbria Copley was able to trace the line of the Roman road from Papcastle to Egremont, as clear as anything; yet on the ground, not a sign. The first signs of dusk were falling on Portsea as they landed, back where they had begun.

Watching the helicopter depart the reality of the situation began to hit hard.

"I expect our phones are being monitored so communicating with Evelyn is going to be difficult. When does Seymour's party join us?"

"First thing in the morning; I haven't been given a cover story, let's face it the students know the sketch; they'll put up with them; they've too much to lose. For our sakes I have given them a good idea of what to wear and bring with them; there won't be a problem with that. A couple of them took Archaeology at Uni"

"Yes. Seymour mentioned it; find out what they can do and we'll put them in a trench well out of the way from us; that's two accounted for; the rest will be shovel and barrow fodder. That'll keep them busy.

I'm off to Brighouse Farm to use the phone; I need to contact Evelyn"

"I bet she's not happy that Sir Seymour Thwaite's is involved; bit of an eye opener that he works for MI6"

"What would you expect, he was a piss poor lecturer and his research was dodgy; who else would get to the top. He didn't even have a doctorate, but his political game playing got him a chair in Byzantine studies at Glasgow and now look at him; they give him the nation's security to play with; bloody farcical.

Anyway, I'm off to ring Evelyn."

"Send her my best regards"

"I won't and you know why"

Copley walked over the rise and down the track to Brighouse Farm; a remote, but charming spot, overlooking the river Esk and the sand dunes, with the sea beyond. The river had gone out to the South of Brighouse until about a thousand years ago; a mixture of longshore coastal drift and a massive storm (Copley considered a possibility of tsunami), event blocked the southerly outpouring, causing the river to flow onto dry land and cut a new course northwards up to Portsea, destroying all in its path, including part of the Roman fort.

Copley was warmly welcomed, and he was soon listening to Evelyn.

"Seymour Thwaites; well there's no surprise there; how else did you think he'd get a knighthood. You've wittered about it long enough; just because you don't have one."

"Yes, but if I got one it would be for services to Archaeology, not blundering around with the countries security.

Any news on my parcel?

"Not yet; it probably hasn't been bundled yet, give it chance. It could take another week or more. Where do you want it sent?"

"I'll come over and deal with it; Ernie can run the show for a day or so; just let me know when it arrives. How is our beloved Vice Chancellor?

"Happy as Larry at the moment; Seymour has, no doubt, been busy with him too. I'd be careful Copley; it doesn't smell good from here."

"Don't worry I will be.

By the way is everything ok for Orkney?"

"I'll keep you informed. Take care."

Copley felt reassured someone was looking out for him and somebody would be on Seymour Thwaite's case; Evelyn would dig the dirt. As for Jeff, he was on his own.

Chapter Three

Jeff had never had any dealings with Copley; the shadowy figure in the office at the end of the department corridor; beyond the library, past all the tutor's rooms and the secretary's office. More a lair for a rare forgotten beast, legendary, Beyond the likes of him. He, knew Copley existed, his smiling face was on all the department literature; as a Fresher he'd seen Copley giving a helping hand to the University CAMRA branch. Copley had also given the introductory department lecture, it had lasted five minutes; and then another lecturer had taken over; that was it. He knew nothing off him until he'd been whisked away. At least Copley had good taste in women; Evelyn. She was something else. She could teach him a lot, she looked and sounded demanding.

Heinrich Stumple, what would he be like? Would he have some answers?

The train glided into in Munich Hbf, the wide concourse shone like a sea and Jeff started his voyage across it, following the signs to the S Bahn. His attention otherwise engaged he didn't take notice of the two police officers approaching him. He didn't resist when they stopped him and asked for his ID; he didn't resist when they took him out of the station into a waiting police car.

The Ettsrasse is shadowed by the prim Augustine gauntness of the Bavarian police headquarters; Jeff found himself escorted into the building and into a lift. He counted the floors; they stopped at the third. The Police had perfect English, but Jeff had merely confirmed his name and had made no attempt to question why he was where he was. He guessed that the pick-up was to do with his reason for being in Munich, but he wasn't giving anything away. He was still in a state of semi shock – stunned by the fact his mission had ended before it had really begun. He was curious; furious and bemused, but curiosity emerged from the haze; yes he was curious. He had broken no law, he was safe, as safe as anyone in a foreign country. This was Germany, what would they do to him; nothing; back in England anything could happen. He'd heard too many stories from fellow students, after a good seeing too from the plod taking it out on pissed up students because nobody would care or know.
Jeff felt more focused as he walked down the corridor; the line of blank doors seemed to constrain his nervousness; the shiny dark floor permitted his passing without a sound.

Jeff was politely gestured into an office where the two policemen escorting him offered a seat, dropped his backpack onto the floor and swiftly left, closing the door behind them. The sun shone through the window; the light played across the empty desk in front of him. The room was empty

"Mr. Blackwell what brings you to Munich?"

The voice appeared from nowhere.

Jeff looked around the room. The voice was coming from the desktop phone; its loudspeaker fizzled.

"Please sit down"

The voice was behind him. The door had opened.

"You will excuse the phone; I am getting used to my new "handi"

The voice was emanating from a distinguished looking suited man. He seemed preoccupied with his mobile; his manner was one of a man in a hurry to be as far away from Jeff and his ilk as possible. They were not of his world.

No ordinary policeman thought Jeff; this was something different, the suit looked too old even to be a policeman – no this was just as the Prof had said – odd.

"Now Mr. Jefferson. Why are you in Munich?"

"I've never been to Munich; opportunity arose, I decided to have a few days…"

"Mr. Jefferson; let us not waste any time on niceties. I believe you are here to see Heinrich Stumple; am I correct?

"I'm on holiday, I…

"Stumple is dead; murdered this morning. We know it wasn't you. So why were you going to see him?

"I don't know what you are talking about."

"Yes. you do. Let me tell you how we found Stumple this morning. In bits. Lots of little bloody bits. Somebody took him apart. Your journey was in vain"

"I'm sorry; I have no idea what this is about."

"You wanted to see Stumple to find something out."

"I don't know Stumple."

"But you know someone that knows him; Hanna Kemp. You dig with her at Portsea; she is a fellow student. You know of her."

"She was in the same department as me at Castletown, I didn't know her.

"Of course, she is dead; blown up I believe"

"Look, whoever you are; I have no idea why I am here, Am I being arrested? If so on what grounds; I know nothing about a guy called Stumple. I do know that Kemp was in my department at University. That's it, nothing else. I came to Munich because…

"Professor Copley sent you."

Jeff was about to reply, when the door opened. The two officers appeared again.

"Take Mr. Jefferson away. This interview is at an end"

A sudden realization that perhaps things were very wrong, and co-operation was the best solution swept across his mind. No, he would remain steadfast.

Without a word he stood up, the officers took him and his bag out of the room. The suit said not a word and returned to his mobile.

The officers escorted Jeff to the lift, which descended five floors; into a sub-basement. Out of the lift into a brightly lit whitewashed garage, where the floors shone back like a pool of mercury. A Mercedes taxi stood with the door open; the officers gestured to Jeff to get in. The door closed and the taxi moved away. Jeff was utterly confused. He noticed the door locks were engaged. He looked back, the officers were gone, the car wound its way out into the open and away from Ettstraße.

Jeff tried to engage the driver, to get out, but the glass screen prevented him from talking to him, the intercom was in the off position. He would just have to sit back and wait his fate. The kilometers went by; the autostrasse took them South. The hours passed. Jeff felt sleepy; the mental stress had caught up. He awoke as the taxi swerved to miss a bicycle, the sign said Berchtesgaden.

The taxi pulled up next to an apartment block, the locks were released. Jeff stepped out.

"Jeff"

"Yes."

"Welcome to Berchtesgaden"

A young very attractive woman was smiling at him. What a contrast to the isolation of the car and the experience in Munich. Jeff was dumb for a few moments; unsure why he was where he was and who or what was going on. He didn't get a chance to speak this lovely lass had taken his hand and drawn him into the door of an apartment block and up the marble staircase to a substantial door. The door open, he found himself in a light and sunny lounge.

"Don't worry you're safe here. Let me take your bag. You must be tired and hungry?"

"I'm sorry, who err where am I?

"My name's Jessica and I'm going to be keeping an eye on you; you're in my flat, that is the Oberslazburg out the window and you have just been rescued by a very nice man; because somebody wanted you locked up in Munich on a trumped up drugs smuggling charge to get you out of the way."

"Do you know Hanna Kemp?

"No. But I know you were sent over to find Heinrich Stumple at EU Freight and the real Hanna Kemp, one Erika Schneider. Look; take it easy, you are with the good guys; even the Police have hidden you away; you could be in Munich in a cell – that's where your Government would leave you until this is over. Relax. Hard I know, but it's going to be ok"

Jeff smiled, he hadn't smiled for a while; it was all a mad nightmare, but Jessica was making it just that little bit more bearable.

Jessica took his bag and he instinctively followed her to his room.

"Help yourself a shower and I'll take you down to the brewery for a meal."

He felt safe, why he didn't know, but he was in a lovely flat, a lovely girl; chance of a shower, food and sleep – tomorrow would be another day. Somebody obviously was interested in his survival let alone the Hanna Kemp business. Jessica had left him alone; he stripped, wrapped the dressing gown around him and headed for the shower.

The steamy hot water trickled his worries away and he physical stretched out, massaging his limbs out; the day had been a long one, a beer and bed. Who was Jessica? It didn't matter at the moment. He'd checked his bag in the taxi, the phones hidden in his socks were still there his contact with Evelyn, his lifeline. He felt at ease.

"Ready"

Suitably refreshed and changed Jeff was ready for anything; well a beer at least, some food and bed.

"Before we go; let's get one thing straight; you are very welcome here, but no questions as to what I'm doing, or why and for whom. Let's just enjoy tonight; you'll like the brewery, and an early night probably after what you have been through. You are a stranger here, we get plenty of tourists, so you're not out of place, you can relax- anybody looking for you thinks you are in a Munich police cell. So come on, cheer up, it could be worse"

And with that Jeff was drawn out of the flat to enjoy an evening in Berchtesgaden.

He would do as he was told and it looked like it would be fun; his head was in a whirl; nothing really seemed to be making sense, but that was what life was about, an adventure.

The brewery in Berchtesgaden a magnificent temple to the art, full of life engulfed Jeff within a moment.

Far above in the frozen waste of the upper atmosphere satellites buzzed with data; no names of the Cumbria tragedy had yet been released; a patient was transferred to London from Castletown for a life-saving operation; the barman was thus being kept very safe – a new life and identity in New Zealand his destination; students were texting that life at Portsea was normal, Ernie was pissed again. A long complex code was being transmitted and it bounced from satellite to satellite, destination a high frequency receiver in Cumbria. Another and another. The night was full of numbers falling like snow.
Below in Cumbria. Copley was wondering what would happen next; far too much excitement for one archaeologist. His reputation would be mired; the rumour mill would be hard pushed to keep up. However, so far, the facts were still pretty clear cut, Copley had nothing to do with any of it. That was all that really mattered. Seymour would also smooth things over, But at what cost? The idea of being at his beck and call was unthinkable.

Ernie had taken the new 'recruits' onboard; fortunately, they seemed to have got the message and they didn't stand out. For once some proper planning and research seemed to have taken place.

After the events of the last few days Copley's attitude to his students had changed. It would be rather useful if they stayed alive. He had been mulling over Ernie's comment about the smashed in face; what could they be trying to do? Perhaps disguise the identity- amateurish, no; not realistic unless you wanted a shor-term advantage; a couple of days and the rest of the forensics available would have worked out who it was.

It was, as Ernie suggested, a case of covering up something. Was it possible to hide something in somebody's face, something you could remove? What would you want to carry that way? Copley was aware of body scanners, he disapproved, they only showed up his penis in glorious Technicolor. But they did show up anything in the obvious orifices. What about the mouth and the nose? Had Ernie got some photos of the body, if he had that might help re the teeth?

Copley shook himself out of his mulling and wondered how Jeff was fairing; what was Evelyn doing sending the lad on such a mission and why had he agreed to it. Simply he did what Evelyn said, most of the time, even if grudgingly; it saved a lot of bother; she was clever; he was just studious, when he wanted to be. He just plodded most of the time; inspiration came at a cost; imagination seemed a tad blurred these days; hardly surprising perhaps.

 "They are managing quite well"

Ernie stopped Copley's musings dead. Reality was a gently steaming archaeologist with a slight attack of BO.

"The Plod?"

"Yes. Surprisingly well, we might actually get some archaeology done"

"Steady lad; would there be some WPCs here?"

"Yes."

"Handcuffs and truncheons, that'll keep you busy."

"Bastard"

"Seriously. Do you think everyone's safe?"

"You worried about students, God, I suppose we must get used to it. We'll have to find some more skirt with knives in them – keep you on the happy side of life."

"How would you like me to stick something up your nose?"
"Steady lad; only kidding"

"No, I'm serious. If you stuck something up your nose, where would it go and how easy would it be to do it; so that you couldn't see it. Can you insert say a capsule into your sinuses?

"Ahh. I see where this is going. You agree that the face was mashed up afterwards?"

"I wondered if you had the photos from the excavation; wondered if she was carrying something like a false tooth."

"Yes, get your drift; but the sinus is a better possibility; you can poke all sorts of things up your nose. Get it wrong and your dead – well at least that's what I think. Suppose it wouldn't do any harm to try the font of all knowledge"

"Evelyn?"

"No, Google. Leave it with me. If I have a look and compare what I find with the photo's – yes I have them on a stick somewhere; you can go and direct the dig and don't just stand on the edge making your usual naff comments; get your hands dirty. You're sure about this aren't you; there's some pretty freaky things going on here. I know that look."

"Yes. My reckoning is this woman was carrying something that was vital to someone and if it was that small it isn't going to be drugs."

Ernie was away to his laptop and Copley to the dig to impress a new audience; the students had heard it all before, but the Plods hadn't, so there was a God. All he had to do was stay alive and where possible make sure others stayed the same way. His gaze was momentarily taken by the jet stream of a plane, high up, over to the West; not many planes came this way; the nuclear site was a no fly zone; a few transatlantic flights would turn late on the beacon, but many miles offshore. All that blue sky and a plane going who knows where; on a journey, on the way to adventure; in reality the humdrum of timetabled existence; but from down on the ground it looked exciting; Copley liked flying; he had enjoyed his trip in the helicopter, even if he had been preoccupied. Looking down at the landscape always enthralled him; so much undiscovered, so much to find.

All Copley could hear was the scraping of metal on earth, a gentle bubble of sound from the pot washing tables and the distant sound of a train crossing the Waynaflud viaduct. Copley was in his element; outside in the fresh air with an audience. For a blissful moment all was very well with the world.

Feeling calm and even, momentarily, content; bordering on happy, a call to Evelyn seemed appropriate, just to put a bit of icing on the cake. He missed her. He used her. No. She could use him. It was about equal.

"Hi gorgeous; missing you"
"You sound in a good mood"

"Cannot complain. A helicopter ride to see Thwaites, a dig full of undercover Plods and a couple of dead bodies – why shouldn't I be happy?"

"We have a package in the South."

"What's it doing there?

"Redirected for us; it's safe, but only because it was picked up for us.

"Well that's the end of that then; it was silly to try."

"Not necessarily"

"Everything else ok; no scandal, no repercussion re me being festooned with bodies?"

"No, Thwaites seems to have poured gallons of oil on troubled waters. He's making it obvious that there is something amiss. Still that's his problem."

"Miss you"

"Copley, behave yourself; I miss you too. What are you up to; you don't sound your normal pompous self?"

"I've got Ernie doing some research for me, so I'm in charge of the site."

"Good grief, you must be ill; are you sure this is wise? Ahh, I know why you're so enthusiastic – it's the undercover cops-you can bore them senseless. Poor devils they don't know what awaits them."

"You can be quite unkind at times"

"Truthful; anyway, take care and see you soon; I'll keep you posted"

"Same to you; just make sure the South is ok."

"I will. Bye"

Copley felt better than he had done in ages; for all the carryings on around him, life was good. A few new students to impress, that would see him right for the rest of the day. He strode off towards the trenches with a skip in his step, he nearly managed a whistle. He hadn't had to ring Evelyn, he had wanted too, he fancied her like crazy, he always had, ever since he had walked into her office and looked at her. There he was his usual; pompous self-opinionated self and she just wiped the floor with him; tidied him up; looked after him and made him feel wanted. He was even getting used to looking different.

No doubt Ernie would be assisted by a student of the female gender in his research, as long as he wasn't stupid enough to let one of the Plod realize what he was doing, all would be well. Copley mused to himself.

The dig was humming along nicely; Ernie had long ago identified the third year and post grads that could look after the trenches; for all his faults Ernie was a very good field archaeologist and his students recognized him for it; he discouraged as many as he could from going into the profession. There simply were not the jobs and the money was crap; Copley was an exception; books and TV were the only way to get on and both required tenacity and the real source of his mottled genius, Evelyn. Universities offered the privileged media encrusted few the glories of residency; no having to plead to survive term to term; favour to favour, siding with the right party and falling when getting it wrong. How many brilliant minds had been lost to archaeology because of the pettiness of others? Copley had met so many, mostly women that, by one means or another, often sexual abuse (as far as Copley was concerned) were dropped like a discarded condom. Copley was master of his craft, he had risen to the top, but had the sense to know that vulnerability is but a knife edge away; that and Evelyn to watch his back and Ernie to do the work for him, leaving him time to manipulate all around him with ease; as long as you understood that academia was a gladiatorial game you stood a chance of survival and a nice little earner, if you played the cards right.

Copley regretted nothing, he had risen, others had fallen by the wayside; he had done his best to quietly assist the fallen, when they had shown worth. He genuinely regretted the demise of many and smiled at others; he could hold a petty squabble and yet admire his adversaries' abilities. He enjoyed the company of fellow malevolent souls.

Archaeology is beyond passion; it is either in you or it is merely a vestment to be cast aside when the temptations of wealth and well-being come upon you. The archaeologist sees beyond today, scrapes away at the edges of the void; opens doors into worlds shadowed and lost. Behind the eyes of an archaeologist lies the witness of all our doings.

Copley shrugged off his dark musings; he wanted to be light and cheery today; the heaviness and responsibilities could be boxed up and filed away for a brief spell. Light and cheery would be a shock for the students; his very presence would equally be a surprise; as he approached the first trench; he noted a few bodies diving down behind spoil heaps and others shrinking on their kneeling mats. He ignored this, he would be pleasant and of course he had novices; Police they maybe, but they were here to learn as far as he was concerned. They were supposed to blend in, he would make sure they did.

"Good morning Professor"
An attractive blond stood up and brushed the soil from her T shirt. Copley, not knowing any of his students that well; but knowing they tended to wash, and dress only occasionally decided that this was a WPC.

"Good morning; settling in, are we? How are we getting on?

Copley looked round for a face he might recognize; fortunately, a third year stood up.

"She's doing very well"

The third year grinned. The blonde grinned back at him. Copley moved on; it was obvious that relations were convivial enough. He headed for the pot washing benches and finds trays; an array of finds were set up on tables outside the main site tent. The one endearing feature of a Roman dig is that there never ever is a shortage of find's. The Romans were the messiest of people, that and the fact everyone around them adopted their throw away lifestyle. Portsea, a major Roman port with a large vicus and transient population was no exception. Post Roman occupation of Portsea saw the fort and vicus abandoned; the port remained in constant use and the major masonry blocks from both fort and vicus left as valuable ballast. The vicus saw a small community, associated with the port; but coastal raiding must have been a constant feature-hence the Bath House survived; thick enough walls and sturdy enough as a strong point to defend for the locals. The Bath House is described in early records as a Palace; compared to the majority of post Roman buildings it was.

Copley had excavated the vicus over many years and knew it intimately; perhaps that was why he had been annoyed with the body's appearance; it had desecrated his life's work. On the other hand, he had become so aware of the place he had not bothered to check his trenches, his work was now distant from him. The body had brought the place back into sharp focus for him. He was errant and he regretted it. Copley gazed over the green fields that made up the vicus today; to the left the Bath house; beyond, further left the early medieval structures lay just beneath the sod; he had once walked the land with his great fiend Sir Patrick Allen; Patrick had lifted an entire wattle and daub wall panel out of the ground; intact as it had fallen. There was no shortage of archaeology at Portsea, you could fall over it every day.

The pottery trays glinted in the sun; freshly washed Samian ware looked as good as the day it was tipped from the dining table onto an unforgiving tessellated floor. Coarser pottery provided a contrast and the glassware offered the finest show of all; beads from Egypt in profusion; perfume phials; jugs and bowls; misty green bubbled glass all foggy and mysterious. Portsea saw trade from all over the Roman world and far beyond.

Copley soaked it all in, he was in his true environment; the academic battleground was a side show, he dwelt in it too much; that and the murders, they were all peripheral to the cause; distractions from the art.

Copley's musings were drawn back to the actual with a start; there really was work, to be done; he was in command and his shoes would get dirty. Mud. It went with the territory and it brushed off; mud was good.

Striding out across the site Copley was drawn to the scene of the murder; the widened section, dug to release the body had proved useful. The murderer had placed the body just short of a cornerstone, by the size it was an impressive structure. From a previous excavation Copley was pretty convinced that this was part of the temple of Claudius. The stonework looked the same; the building had stood for a long time in the Cumbrian elements, the stone was ornate, the carving quite delicate and formal, but blurred by centuries.

Copley touched the stone.

He listened.

The tramp of feet as cohort marched up to the fort, the traders exchanging insults; the hammers singing in the blacksmiths shop; the priest deep in conversation with the brothel keeper next door; the rumbling of carts and moaning oxen on their way North.

He Looked. Noted the detail of the shop fronts with their pillared arcades, all frontage with a simple interior and living quarters beyond; the fountain and the smoke and steam escaping from the Bath houses; a wine is awaiting you at the bar and a game of dice. Officers from the fort at Galava getting drunk with the architect of the new market who should be supervising the workers replacing the drains, yet again. Shoppers complaining to the traders about the prices of figs; dogs chasing the rats and sailors threatening a strike over late paid wages.
A pigeon drops a message on the statue of Claudius and a girl, basket of berries in hand stops to stroke a goat idly chewing on a sailor's tunic as he lay drunk in the gutter.

He understood. The earth tingled beneath his feet, he breathed long and hard a deep silent swelling of eternal breath; the traveller of worlds taking the flood as a mere stream, to cross and cross again.

Copley's picture vanished. A student appeared as if from out of the earth to his left.

"Professor Copley have a look at this."

The student handed over a minute silver pill like container, or at least half of one, it shone in the sunlight. Copley looked hard, the metal was unusual to the touch; whilst it glinted it wasn't chrome, or steel.

"Where did this come from?"

"Here."

The student pointed to the left of where Copley was standing. The student had been working right next to him and he had been lost in his other world, he had been oblivious, as ever. So much for his attention to the job at hand.

"Just about twenty centimetres below where the body was found."
Copley turned the capsule over in his fingers. Copley mused for a moment; it could be a vital clue; a small titanium capsule, hidden in the girl's sinus, removed with a scalpel and then the face deliberately smashed in to cover any traces. It was a real possibility. Ernie had considered the facial injuries to be an after-thought. How could it be under the body? Unless the person that had extracted the capsule also took whatever was in it and merely threw the shell away and then dropped the body on top. A careless act, or deliberately casual; with forensics and archaeology going on it would be bound to be found. To smash a face up to hide the cause of death, but there again, all the murder had done was slow the process of discovery down; burying the body in an obvious place with people that would know how to cope with such a challenge was equally a case of couldn't care less. There was a taste of inevitability, perhaps even broadcasting some message, something that couldn't be stopped.

"Thanks, good job. Is it fully recorded?
Finds bag and reference number and back to me with it.
ASAP"

Copley worked his way out of the trench without further ado, leaving the student to carry out his command. Where was Ernie when you needed him, it all was coming together, but what it was; well that had even Copley puzzled?

Bertschegaden Hbf and a tall well-dressed woman alighted from the train from Freislang junction; she made her way out of the side entrance, along the busy road to Salzburg, then left, past the Hotel Bavaria and left again onto the path behind the cemetery; arriving at the apartment block next to the church.

The door lock buzzed, the door swung open, her heels clicked on the marble steps. She put her keys in the lock and entered the hallway of the apartment.

"Hello Mummy".

"Hello darling. Where is he?"

"Sleeping off his woes, in the spare room; I took him to the brewery last night, got him a meal and a few beers, but he was still shaken up from the business in Munich. It's a good thing you have your friends there, God knows what would have happened"

The woman removed her coat and slowly opened the spare room door. Jeff was asleep, the bed hardly ruffled, he had fallen into a deep sleep the moment his head had touched the pillow.

"Good morning Jeff"

Jeff stirred.

"Good morning"

Jeff's eyes opened, there was a look of complete panic, then confusion, then school boy modesty as he pulled the bedclothes towards him.

"Evelyn"

"Good morning. Don't worry, get yourself in the shower, breakfast will be ready when you're out of it. Go on, off you go.

Jeff lay there, stunned.

"Come on Jeff, there's work to be done. A run in with the Police isn't going to stop you. Is it?

Jeff muttered that it wasn't

Evelyn, knowing only too well how the male of the species required to raise itself from the Neanderthal state threw a dressing gown at him and left him to it. Men were strange creatures, so easily pleased; it took years to train them to please women. Evelyn smiled to herself; Jeff was an innocent; just as Copley had been. Copley had been brave and confident; he still was both, but he now needed her. She liked that, she liked that a lot.

Emerging freshly shaved and smartly dressed Jeff prepared to meet the day . He was utterly amazed, first the Police then the lovely Jessica and now Evelyn. What was Evelyn doing here?

"I hope my daughter is looking after you well?"

Jeff sat down at the balcony table wide eyed.

"Don't look so shocked; though I suppose it is a surprise that Copley managed to produce such a well-balanced sensible daughter, with none of his attributes. Well none that she will admit to me.

I'm sorry you were put through that business in Munich; I had a call to warn me that you were going to be picked up; fortunately, the German police don't like being told what to do by our MI6; Seymour Thwaites is an arrogant bastard at the best of times and I persuaded a few friends to spirit you out of harm's way. If MI6 ask, you are still in Munich under lock and key.

It was a chance. We took it and now they think we have failed."

"They think?"

"Good grief, you don't think we give up that easily. Thwaites and his compatriots will think so; Copley is being watched by half of Special Branch; you are supposed to be in a Munich jail. The last thing anybody is going to think is we will go after Heinrich Stumple."

"He's dead. The guy in Munich told me. Cut to pieces. Murdered"

"I don't think so. I spoke to him this morning at the railway station. Flesh and blood all intact!

"Where is he then?"

"Here."

"Sorry, not with you. I'm still trying to come to terms with the fact I'm sitting here in the first place."

"In Berchtesgaden. Stumple has no great desire to be in the presence of the Police, he has been the subject of people smuggling allegations, nothing proved, but he knows when it's best to keep a low profile. They were trying to frighten you to see if you reacted when they told you he was dead. I suspect you looked shocked. They were looking for a reaction"

"You knew this when you sent me to see him?"

"Yes. I also knew that MI6 would be trailing after you, courtesy of Thwaites, that the German authorities would be less than sympathetic to the Brits because it was going to screw up their enquiries regarding Stumple and people smuggling. We were a side show for them, so getting you out of the way was easy. Let's face it nobody would expect Stumple to be here under the circumstances."

"But wouldn't they be bugging Stumple's phone; surely they know where he is?"

"When I initially made contact, I kept it clean as a whistle; then two hours later Stumple received, by courier, a mobile phone which I then rang with a suggestion of a way out. He took it. He's no fool."

Jeff looked at the pair of them, head spinning. How had Copley managed it? There was more to the Professor than met the eye. Beautiful wife and daughter and frankly everything else. How?

"Where is he?"

"In the Edelweiss, room 34."

Jessica poured Jeff an orange juice.

He looked at her, smiled and grinned.

"I don't think I can keep up with this; whatever happens next, I don't care, I just am going to go along with the flow. I'm just happy to be here rather than a Munich jail cell and as long as I can stay out of one, I don't mind what I do."

Evelyn couldn't help smiling. Jeff was sounding like Copley. He was learning fast.

Chapter Four

Copley leaned over the microscope; one thing about Ernie, he had all the right kit. The digital light source and camera helped examine finds in extremely fine detail and this find was getting Copley's full attention.

The capsule, or to be precise half of it was the size of any proprietary heart pill. The idea of that up the nose would have made life painful, but not impossible. Getting it into the sinus would have been messy. The patient would have to be sedated and it would be a bloody business via the nose; so more likely through the roof of the mouth, with a stitch or two to keep it in place. What puzzled Copley was the fact it hadn't been detected by the metal detectors at the airport; the metal needed an expert's eye.

Overhead he heard a jet.

Odd thought Copley, second one today that has turned westward as close as this to Pentland Nuclear.

The sound of an excavation; of hand toothbrushes on pottery, the gentle occasional banter of the students bent over their work, the measuring; the photography. Much had changed since Copley had first got his hands dirty over fifty years ago. As a lad he'd been lowered into the depths of Iron Age hillforts ditches on ropes; no shoring; just the weight of ages on earth holding the side up. With instructions to gently brush the surface to ready it for photography. A time when drawing was a proper art and photography was expensive and thus carried out with extreme care. An age when observation was scrutiny, time was taken. True, with the digital age this could be done afterwards and perhaps more was now discovered, but their link with sight touch and location; that was still primary. The capsule perplexed Copley; he was wondering exactly what he had got and whether he should let Thwaites in on the game. No. He would not. Nothing about Thwaites made Copley feel willing to cooperate, unless there was a straightforward return. something about Thwaites stunk and for once it was not professional rivalry.

Had any of the spooks noticed what he was doing?

Copley walked over to the pottery washers and chose a particularly ordinary piece of coarse ware; he took it over to the viewer and popped it onto the stand. Copley then left the tent. Giving himself some distance and with the cover of the toilet block he turned and looked back. Sure, enough one of Thwaites spooks went into the finds tent. A few minutes later he came out again; obviously none the wiser.

Copley smiled to himself. It was a small victory. Copley liked small, private victories. Learning at an early age that personal satisfaction took many forms. He revelled in getting the better of others. Perhaps? No. Definitely. Yes. The result of others, thinking they had got the better of him. He'd had the last laugh. Oh yes. The last laugh.

Copley is eighteen, he's out with his college pals; the beer is flowing. The talk is of women and sex. Copley's no virgin. That went long before, but he finds himself the butte end of a joke involving a pretty barmaid. The barmaid is more than capable of putting a bunch of posh boys in their place. Words are exchanged and before the group are told to sling their hook, they leave.

Copley steps back into the pub to apologize. The barmaid responded very favourably to his apology and she suggests he stay and leave the kids to their own devices. Copley encouraged, stays at the pub and leaves with the barmaid at the end of her shift. He remembers her smile, her breasts, her laugh, He felt comfortable, she was probably only two years older than him. Copley couldn't remember her name; he could remember everything else. But not that.

Copley arrived at the barmaids flat and the drawing over the threshold with a warm kiss and the promise of more than a coffee had needed no further encouragement. Copley was onto a winner.

Into a comfortable small lounge and cuddles on the sofa; nothing more than lightly mauling each other; exploring each other's curves and kissing technique. The delights of nakedness and discovery were likely as not to follow, Copley was eager. Copley was a bag of nerves.
Clothing for both was intact if ruffled in readiness for removal as the barmaid drew him towards a pink door which Copley fully anticipated was a bedroom.
Beyond the door, beyond that threshold Copley's world was to change forever.
The walls.
They were jet black. Where you could see the walls.
 Chains, leather paddles, masks.

Copley was transfixed. Copley's mind went to another level; not fear, not bravado, inquisitive, Yes. Definitely. Inquisitive. He took in the sight, observing the buckles, zips and the boots. The boots. Long shiny spiked boots. Black, red; white and pink. Boots into which women, this woman no doubt would zip herself. Oh yes. Oh God this was paradise.

No bed. But a gynecologists chair and a leather padded stool with two medical wheeled trolleys; one containing an array of tubing and syringes; the other a range of ever increasing dildos.

Copley closed the door behind him. Symbolically stating his intent. He was in. What ever happened next. All fear of not coming up to scratch had vanished. He was the pupil, expected to learn and he was oh so willing.

The barmaid seemed encouraged by the ever-increasing bulge in Copley trousers. She stroked it. She gripped him by the trouser belt, drawing Copley to her lips. She looked into his eyes. Copley was hers. Copley would do anything to see her in those boots, the leather the latex. She could do anything to him. This was paradise.

"Shower"

She pointed to the door adjacent and Copley proceeded as commanded. He stood under the sharp pummeling jet, his erection undaunted by the soap and water. A new phase of Copley's life was opening. He would accept it and learn. He was going to enjoy. Delve into the leather, delve into his inner self and explore where his mind and wrist had taken him so oft before.

"Leave your clothes on the hangers"

Copley duly obeyed and stepped naked back into the room.

The barmaid was now dressed in nothing but a pair of pink thigh high boots with accompanying basque and large shiny strap on cock; pointing threateningly at Copley. Copley's gaze would have centred on her, but for the fact there was now another woman in the room, A tall brunette, only identified as such by the plume of a pony-tail forced through the top of a head mask. This magnificent woman was dressed head to tail in red shiny latex with boots that rubbed against the zip covering her cunt.

Copley was transfixed.

"On your knees"

The brunette spat the words at Copley. She meant it.

Copley obeyed and instinctively looked at the floor. An ex public schoolboy, knowing the drill; knowing to accept humiliation and a pummelling. Unlike the past Copley was sucking the whole thing in with delight. It was like opening a door to a new World; he was anticipating new vistas.

There followed a brief verbal list of instructions that Copley duly accepted, he would have done anything, he was on a high of curiosity and rampant sexual desire. With a nod of the head he willingly succumbed and was instructed to lick the brunette's cunt. Heaven. Half an hour with his tongue inside her, playing with her clit. His nose rubbing against her lips taking in her smell and the smell and texture of the latex and the leather of the boots. Her juices were flowing, Copley instinctively knew a command was coming to desist. It came. He was ordered to suck the strap on which was slid into his mouth; whilst his back and shoulders were paddled. The slicing pain of a cane ripped into his arse. His cock grew even stiffer. Bliss. Pure bliss.

Ordered to lie in the 'gyny' seat, Copley's erection was subject to much handling and the barmaid, removing her strap on, mounted him. Copley felt the muscles inside her grip him, then sliding herself fully onto him   syphoning Copley deeper into her. The brunette began tonguing Copley's ball sack. Such activity would normally have the desired outcome. Not this time. Copley was on another level. He wasn't ready to let go of anything. He was on another planet. This was better than grass or even beer. This was a drug he really could get into. The barmaid was almost primeval. Copley could feel her muscles pulsing and contracting. Seeing her friend's over exuberance the brunette curtly ordered her off Copley, the barmaid wanted more, but a glance from the brunette saw the barmaid lift herself off Copley's glistening cock. The brunette licked Copley's cock savouring her friend's juices and then proceeded to deep throat him. Copley responded by thrusting his cock deeper into her mouth, his balls against her chin. She was just able to breathe through her nose. She wanted to taste her success, he would oblige but when he was good and ready none of his cum was going anywhere yet. Copley realised that these two professionals were at the very least impressed with his staying power.

The barmaid was beneath the brunette slowly licking her cunt, while she continued sucking Copley's steadfast erection. The barmaid fingers quickly playing with her own cunt. The brunette stopped sucking Copley and let out an orgasmic groan; her hand gripping Copley's cock so hard he nearly lifted from the chair.

The barmaid lowered the 'gyny' chair flat and proceeded to sit on Copley's face, facing him. Her cunt in his mouth, wet juicy; if she pressed forward, he could hardly breathe. The brunette now straddled his cock. She slid down onto it in one slow accepting moment.

This was the life. Thought Copley. He was looking forward to much more of this.

It was obvious Copley or to be precise his constant erection was proving a pleasant surprise. He was compliant. Men were little boys that needed spanking and their wallets draining. But that cock was still firm after the pasting and that amused and pleasured them. He could have some more.

Copley breathed through his nose, his mouth and tongue occupied; lustily sucking the barmaid, her body melting in his mouth.

The brunette snatched at Copley's nipples, twisting them hard. She rose and fell on him, harder and harder. Copley could feel her body ripple to the motion of her down thrust. His balls being beautifully squeezed by it. She then pulled clear; Copley's cock was throbbing but still stiff despite its vigorous workout. Copley could hear her beginning to remove her latex costume, she was unzipping her boots.

The barmaid, taking advantage of Copley's vacant cock, lifted off his face allowing Copley to gasp some fresh air. She skewered herself onto his cock her boots either side of his face. Copley could see the brunette's wonderful body, shining in sweat, the juices around her shaved cunt glistened. The boots lay on the floor.

"Please mistress, put the boots back on? "

The first words Copley had said. It was shattering a glass wall. Entering a new realm for Copley. The boots were the icing on the cake, he enjoyed his cake with icing.

The brunette smiled at Copley. Looked at the barmaid knowingly. All men
had their weaknesses. They could have a lot of fun with him.

The barmaid lifted herself off Copley and patted his cock and walked to the bathroom, leaving Copley with the brunette. Her breast dangling over Copley as she leaned over him. He licked them.

The brunette stood and walked to the wall, taking down a pair of pink boots. Walking in front of Copley she slowly put them on; stepping into the heal and bending forward to zip herself up. She stopped.

"Zip me up darling; there's a pet"
Copley duly complied.
"Now get over here and face me."
Copley stood in front of this booted goddess. The pink boots reached her crotch, the thighs encased in pink shiny latex.

"You are rather good at this; still nice and stiff aren't we; enjoy all this stuff?
She pointed at the array of equipment.
"Eighteen. Lots of spunk in you. Lots of staying power."
She stroked his cock.
She stroked it a bit more. She rubbed it against her boots.
Backwards and forwards between her thighs.

"Now come"

It was an order.

Copley came.
A jet of spunk flew over the brunette's latex covered thighs, her hands.
He jerked and came again.
He trembled and roared. His whole existence was coming out of him. It was good. So good.
The brunette licked her fingers.
"Now lick that all up."
Copley knelt and duly licked himself up.

"Your friends stitched you up darling; more fool them, bunch of posh snotty bums. You really are good you know. That's not just me trying to get you to see me again. You really are good."

My names Alice. Stephanie is waiting for you in the shower. I think you will be staying the night with her. I sleep alone.

What's your name?

Copley. Everyone just calls me Copley.
"Well Copley if you want to try anything here and you're open to absolutely anything, No hang ups?

Copley affirmed.

"Then you can come here when I command you; if it works out you can be part of the team. Because you are one rock steady young man.

"Now. Stephanie is waiting. See you soon Copley,"
With that the brunette kissed him on the forehead and left the room.

The shower beckoned. Copley looked about the room, tasted the women on him, the leather, the latex; the buckles, chains, tubes, masks,

Heaven.

If only the lads knew what they had done? The biggest favour anybody could possibly have. A gateway to explore their sexual desires and fantasy's; learning in safe capable, practical and funny hands. Laughter amongst the dildos and vibrators.

Copley thought to himself. If only his colleagues knew how he'd funded his way through to his doctorate.

Then he'd met Evelyn; he'd told her all, because he knew he could hide nothing from her. She had just smiled and taken him to her bed wearing a pair of pink thigh boots.

The sound of students deep in discussion of the significance of a foundation layer brought Copley back from his reverie. The past was another place, a safe haven, He had been young once. Lived in another World. He had lived. He was still very capable in the bedroom. Evelyn kept him in trim. Oh the joy of a life partner that really likes to experiment and laugh in the sack.
Copley wasn't going to give in doing so. Desire for the different was part of him and that fuelled sexual passion as well as professional ability, his steadfastness his love for Evelyn, an honest selflessness; covered by layers of pompous armour, was as strong as the first time he held her in his arms.

Archaeology time. His second great love and it was time he took notice of what Ernie and the students had done, allowing for dead bodies, explosions and MI6 goons. Minor inconveniences to any archaeologist worth their salt.

Copley was back to the grindstone. One that he had shaped nicely for himself, admittedly with considerable assistance from Evelyn.

Chapter Five

Jeff, fully refreshed after a good breakfast was enjoying the view; below him the railway station, the road to Salzburg; the river competing for the valley bottom and across the valley the Obersalzburg, towering up festooned with trees and hotels, half hidden by the verdant branches.

Jessica came and sat on the balcony with him; Evelyn could be heard tapping away on a laptop. She would be running the department as if she was there; that and no doubt influencing world events at the same time. Here was her very attractive daughter Jessica; could it get any better? Two very attractive women, very persuasive intelligent women, women that given half a chance Jeff would like to get to know very much better. His mind was beyond racing ahead; the past few days had shattered any sense of reality; one thing he did know; he was going to enjoy whatever happened, because it was a true adventure and with these two it was going to be one hell of a ride – if he was lucky perhaps in more ways than one. He was kidding himself, they would eat him for breakfast, but perhaps he would rather like that. Yes perhaps he should just take whatever came his way. What other choice did he have; he was young and eager to learn whatever was on the menu to take advantage of.

"Mummy has arranged for you to see Stumple this afternoon; she's got the hotel staff keeping an eye on him. We will be off in the car in twenty minutes. We are going to Salzburg."

Jeff was still taking in the view. It certainly was a contrast to Portsea and a smelly ex army tent.

"Fine by me. I'm open minded as to what he has to tell us. I'm surprised he's willing to talk, Especially with the authorities breathing down his neck. What do we know of these far right groups? I mean are they just a bunch of fascist thugs?"

"You're in Germany, Southern Germany. A highly conservative culture allied to the fact Austria is just in front of your gaze. Both countries are now highly critical of the use of nuclear power. The Austrians have been fighting to stop the British building new power stations for years. The German government has taken longer to come round, but the nuclear industry is a dead duck; all the stations are to close. The far right is becoming a legitimate force in Austria and its gaining ground in Germany."

"Why would a group of facist terroists be plodding around in Britain?"
"That's why we need to speak to Stumple?"

"Is your Mother coming along. Would make sense to have her?"

"No. Mother knows she's watched."

"Who by"

"Who not."

"Why"

"Mummy has always oiled the wheels; Daddy says she's very special. She is. She runs his department like clockwork, She can be dealing with a frightened pregnant student one moment and speaking with the Russian Cultural Attaché the next. Everyone knows Evelyn. But she has always been there for me.

Why do you think Daddy is the top dog in his field and spends half the year abroad? Mummy of course. She has a way with her. People just open up to her.
Come on. We better be going. The car will be waiting."

They made their way to the street and a black Mercedes was waiting. The car eased through the streets onto the Salzburg road. Then pulled into the petrol station and round to the autowasher and stopped at the wheels of the washer, Jessica took Jeff's hand and opened the door as the car was about to go into the washer. Around the back of the washer a Golf was waiting. Jessica got into the driving seat and slowly pulled away from the petrol station, Taking the road to Konigsee she checked the rear mirror and smiled.
"Just in case we were being shadowed. Mummy says you can never be too careful and we do have the German Intelligence Service watching and goodness knows whom else."
Jessica pulled into what had been the railway station car park. Parked and walked Jeff into the village; full of tourists heading to the lake. They entered the Hotel Königssee. A brief word with reception and they headed up to Room 14. A crisp knock of the door and Stumple let them in.

Jeff saw Heinrich Stumple. A man that looked perfectly healthy considering he was supposed to be dead according to the Munich Police.

"Hello Jeff. Welcome to Konigssee. Come through. Look at the view. May I get you a drink. A beer. Wine for you Jessica?"

A man in his early fifties, broad but not fat, muscle, from working in the freight business thought Jeff.

They walked through to look out of the window, not out onto the balcony' Konigssee was busy beneath them; the boat dock was a scene of Chinese tourists dutifully waiting the boats. The gift shops were busy and the smell of food rose like a cloud.

"So how can I help you?
 Stumple seemed affable and very calm.

Drinks duly prepared; capacious three=seater sofa beckoning, the three sat looking out into the blue.

"Call me Martin. I'm getting used to it. I've accepted my name is going to change so I might as well get used to it; everything else will be changing too. But it's better than being dead."

"Like Hanna Kemp?"

"Ahh. The reason I must vanish. Everybody wants me to vanish. Strangely I don't mind. I've had a life in freight, heavy haulage. I could do with a change. Enough is enough. No family. Wife left me for her girlfriend ten years back. Good for her. A little bar in Hamburg will do me. With a few rooms upstairs and a couple of working girls to pay the rent and keep me warm in my dotage. Ha. That will do me.
You have no idea about Schneider.

Schneider was a fruitcake, but a funny one; anti-nuclear. Nothing unusual in Germany. The Green Party have us by the balls. Me. I don't care how we turn the lights on. But Schneider took things seriously. She was in with a bunch of NAZI lunatics in Munich. In English they would be the Green Swastika; energy from the pure land of Germany. They see nuclear as a pestilence created by Jewish engineers and communists. All part of the conspiracy to destroy Germany and its rightful place as the master race of Europe. Erika. I don't think that was her real name. Believed all that shit. She would distribute the material all over Europe; pamphlets, arrange local meetings. Hanna was her lover. She swung both ways. Hanna came here, to this very room in fact. I met them for Christmas last year. When Erika wasn't spouting shit, she was a good laugh. Hanna was good for her.

The sound of boats disembarking rose from the dock outside. The sun shone. The three stared, listened and sipped their drinks.

"It was on that holiday we went walking over to the Dokumentaion Centre; the snow was crisp, a good hike and I was all for popping into the International for a gluwein, but Erika insisted there was something she wanted to show me, before we could get warm and snug.

Just to left of the Dokumentation Centre there's a patch of woodland. Deep in the snow, hidden from sight is the foundation of a building. Not much more than a mountain hut. The wood is thick enough to keep the worst of the snow off, so the base was pretty clear. Erika starts kicking the snow off one corner. Gets down on her knees scrabbling the snow away. We just help her. Neither of us asked what she was doing. We laughed.

Then we hit some solid wood. Floorboards. No. We get the outline of a door. A trapdoor. The cellar. You should have seen Erika's face. She knew this was here. We were just curious. Yes. We tried to open it and it did open; because the hinges were greased. I was aware this must have something to do with the Green Swastika, but it was quite exciting, an adventure. We open the door and there's a ladder down into the depths. Concrete lined shaft. All painted and with a light switch at the top. Not exactly derelict. Erika starts down and we follow. Why not. Nobody had been there before us that day, so we weren't going to be bumping into any of her friends. Erika tells me to close the hatch. I wasn't so happy about that, but I did. We must have climbed down twenty metres. At the bottom we arrived in a corridor with a rusty tram track running down the middle, lights glowing. On the adjacent wall is a sign. To the left Control Centre, to the right Secure Area. We headed to the secure area. We must have walked for quarter of an hour. There were man-carriers just lying where the last riders had left them. Tools neatly stacked. Empty packing case. One of them was in English.

"Did you notice what it said?"

"Pentland. Pentland Project Office. In clear red ink. Anyway. We pass through some open gates past a wooden sentry box, so we are entering the secure zone and as we do the lights go out. Pitch black. Really terrifying black.
"Don't worry. It's the time switch."
Erika turns on her walking torch and head a few steps back to the sentry box and the lights go back on. We turn the corner in the corridor, I tell you I've never seen a cavern anywhere in Germany like it. It's vast. The lights were going on, one by one, it just gets larger and larger. Vast. Worth the effort. There's a huge steel tower, a lift shaft going through the cavern roof, next to it a massive concrete platform with gantry. At the end of that is a cradle.

She goes off on one "The British have it. Our nuclear bomb. Our technology. The Americans may have got to Bertchesgaden first, but the British got this away from under their noses. Cunning. I salute them for that. Well we will harvest their ingenuity to our ends. The time is coming"

I thought, here she goes again, off on one of her fascist rants, but it was obvious something of incredible complexity had been in this space. We walked around for a bit, tourists. Awe inspiring. Everything just as it had been until 1945.
Erika then leads us away from the cavern and into a small ante chamber with a pool; least we thought it was a pool. She walks us along the edge of it; she steps into the water and jumps up and down. Then steps back out of the water.

"This is the bit the British never found."

There was a gushing of air, a vibration through our feet; the pool was being sucked away in front of us. Where Erika had jumped was a large metal pad. Beyond it rising out of the pool bed was a lift cage. Black and menacing. I've never seen anything like it. The water ran off it in silver rivulets.
"Come on, it's quite safe, don't touch the wall they are thickly greased. The floors sound. Off we go. Erika turned a big handle on the back wall and there was this rush of air and the whole lift slowly slipped below where the pond had been. We must have dropped a hundred metres. Pitch black. It was terrifying. Then into brilliant light. Jessica was in Erika's arms in an embrace. I felt a bit sick.

"Sorry. No light in that one. But it's worth it. Come on"

A wide corridor, offices, mess room, workshops, laboratories. All standing silent; untouched.

"The Americans and the British never found this."

We walked towards a red door. Two sentry boxes and a table. The ink pad and rubber stamp were still there along with the entry book. Just abandoned. Erika reached into her pocket and took out a small key. Placed it in the lock and this huge door opened inwards without her even touching it. Incredible engineering. German engineering. A small room compared to everything else we'd seen. Just two racks of glass boxes. Inside the boxes were more glass boxes and I could see inside them was yet another. Something very precious, very dangerous lurked in that glass. There were no signs outside, no coat hooks for special clothing, masks or equipment. I just knew that we were in a room with an immensely dangerous something. I could smell carnage. Everything else was just incredible. This terrified me. More than the lift.

"The British took our bomb. Fools. If only they knew. We have risen again. We will wipe the smile off their faces. We will show them what happens when they mess with the Fatherland. Steal our technology. You will pay. We will purify with a fire of justice"

Up to then I'd been ok with our visit. It was difficult to take in; the scale, the elaborate means of concealing whatever it is. It's not very big but whatever it is isn't very nice. I was glad to be back in the fresh air and attached to a very large gluwein.

"Don't you think it odd that all this facility lying there would have been discovered before. How was the power still on.? Jeff turned and looked at Jessica; trying to fathom the story.

"The NAZI party was hated in Bertchegaden, especially by those who lost their property; but times change. I've no doubt some of the local are Green Swastika supporters; the time switch on the light circuit would be enough to deter some; I'm certain that we would never have reached the cavern without something happening. We were being allowed to see what we saw; Erika was showing off to her friends. I suppose she was trying to get me on board. Jessica already knew of Erika's involvement. Erika never said another word when we got back to the surface about it. Never said another thing regarding it the whole holiday. I wasn't going to say"

"Never tried to recruit you."

"No. But she knew I wouldn't say anything. Until now. You know what? I think she deliberately showed me, so she had a witness, somebody that would tell the story I've just told you. I couldn't fathom it at the time. Ok, she trusted me to keep my mouth shut, But; she so easily could have killed me, or got somebody to do it. But until you started poking around, I was perfectly safe. Now I'm in for an identity change and a new address."

"Not because of us I assure you. We are in this as deep as you. If not more so. You know the circumstances of Erika's body being found in the trench at Portsea and Jessica being blown up within hours. You know of the identity swap?"

"I'm sure that was something to do with smuggling and the contents of those glass boxes. Green Swastika gets its funds from, let's say, diverse sources. There are some big backers, but the everyday money comes from drugs, prostitution and smuggling. So much for the pure Germany! That's about all I can tell you. Other than I would like to stay alive to enjoy Hamburg."

The sun shone. A silence fell. The story sank in.

Jessica broke the silence.

"Well thank you Martin. Have you your papers on you. Passport?

Martin nodded.

"A van is waiting for you at the backdoor; put this vis vest on. Nobody takes any notice of people with vis vests. Go out through the kitchen. The van's got a large St Christopher hanging on the dashboard and the driver's got a red beard. You can't miss him. Have a lovely holiday. See you in Hamburg in a year's time"

Martin laughed out loud.

"Your Mother is incredible. Thank her for me. She is a saint."

Martin stood. They all shook hands, quite formally. And without more than a moment to check to find his passport Martin was gone. Leaving his few remnants of occupation of room 19 behind him.
"Well we have the rest of the day to ourselves and quite a lot to take in." Jeff was in serious mood

"Let's go for a trip on Konigssee."

Jeff smiled. He had decided on a much more enjoyable way of passing the hours. There was a hotel room going begging. No. A trip on a boat in the sunshine with the lovely Jessica was just fine. Evelyn could wait for the information on Stumple. He mused to himself that he wouldn't be surprised if she already knew it. Jessica could have a hidden microphone on her. He would have to search her for it.

The couple made their way to the boat dock where one of the boatmen greeted Jessica with a low courteous bow. Jeff was expecting to wait for the next passenger boat. The boatman lifted his hand and into the dock a magnificent launch glided in.

"Thank you, Michael. Mummy sends her regards. We will be out for five or six hours, if there's a problem I'll ring you from the lodge. Come on Jeff. Time to show you Konigssee."

With that Jeff was aboard and they were away.

"I suppose I'm not going to get this question answered, but how does your Father afford all this. Actually. That's not really the right question. Who is Copley? I mean all these people, these people doing things. Your Mother, she's ... who is she? I just know her as the department secretary."

"She is. She supports Daddy. But I imagine you've hardly ever seen her; except during the first couple of weeks of a new term and for Daddy and his excavations. Mummy is busy elsewhere."

"I gathered that. I didn't think much of Professor Copley."

"Pompous old fart. Most students think that. It's ok. I know. He can be, but he sees things, he observes and looks at landscapes like no one else. All sorts of landscapes, for all sorts of people. He gets asked for his opinion and gets rewarded accordingly. Jeff. Relax. Enjoy the scenery. I'm their daughter and I certainly don't know a quarter of what they do. All I know is I trust them with my life, I love them. When they say, I know to do. And. Before you say anything about letting Mummy know about Stumple's story, she already knows."

"You were miked up. I knew it."

"Well done Jeff. You're getting the hang of it. Don't worry. I've switched it off. It's just us two and the view; let's have some lunch; I know a very good place, well the only one. The lodge at Saint Bartholomew's; those distant domes, as you said we do have the rest of the day to ourselves."

The launch cut through the water; silver waves cutting to the shore, an effortless progress. The majesty of the mountains on all sides. Twenty minutes passed and St Bartholomew's welcomed the pair. And they were duly whisked by attentive staff to the private first floor dining room at the lodge.

Whilst Jessica was starting to feel hungry, her primary reason for suggesting lunch was to find out a bit more about Jeff; not just what Evelyn had told her. She was aware that Jeff found her attractive and his unconscious gazing into her eyes and then glancing down to her breasts had certainly not gone unnoticed.

She was certainly no pushover, she had both Evelyn and Copley to thank for that. She had been brought up to have a healthy respect for her body as well as her mind.
She had enjoyed several intimate relationships with young men at university and had even had a brief affair with a lecturer there, although not hers. She'd never had a very lengthy relationship; six months to a year if that. It suited her. She was, after all, still young and there was much to sample of life.
Her parent's relationship, although certainly not conventional, worked.
Evelyn was strong, immensely able and loving and had managed the juggling of a child, relationship and career exceptionally.

The fact that her father had not been around a great deal while she was growing up had not worried, or left her feeling as if she'd missed out.
It had shown her from an early age that a woman can be happy and successful without having a man around all the time.

Jeff appeared keen and she was certainly open to some male company.

Lunch had gone well. Conversation was varied. University, favourite holiday destinations.
After desert and as coffee arrived Jeff suddenly put his hand on hers.
She looked directly into his eyes and slowly stood up from the table.

" I've settled the bill"

Jeff had been attempting to extract his wallet to pay.

There was something in the pocket.

A piece of paper.

Chapter Six

"The road is open. The scum will descend."

Ernie interrupted Copley's train of thought with news he
didn't really want to hear. Copley was aware the road had
been partially cleared to allow the residents of Portsea access,
but the Police had been keeping movement to a minimum and
keeping the Press out as much as they could. British Transport
Police had been busy on the coast train discouraging the Press.
Now it would be open house and the site would be swamped
with media all looking for Copley. Least that is how Copley
saw it.

"Time to make myself scarce. Just make sure the students
know how to deal with this. It's an important part of their
education in the profession. Knowing how to work with the
Press. Ernie. I mean this. Keep it all together. I appreciate what
you do. I don't often say it; but I couldn't do any of this
without you"

"No; you couldn't, now piss off and let me get on. Where you
scurrying to this time?"

"Not far. Back in a day or so"

Copley grabbed his ever-ready travelling case and headed for
the station. Normally he would be the first to welcome media
attention. This time it was to be avoided at all cost. A ticket to
Lancaster. A ticket to Carlisle. Then across to Newcastle. That
would keep anyone trailing him guessing. At Newcastle he
boarded a late train to Kings Cross, certain as anybody could
be that he had no shadow.

Copley sat looking out into the Summer night, he picked at his dinner; a reasonable white wine; a few passengers in the dining car and none that looked as if they were in anyway interested in him,

"St James's Palace please"

Copley was heading for his London address. It was past midnight, but London continued to lurch along. Copley hated it all, its only purpose for him was money to keep him digging and the extrusion of power from others. A vile hole. A pit The taxi stopped by the gates and Copley shadowed by the taxi alighted. The security satisfied that Copley was Copley opened the side door and he walked into the safest apartment in London. Glad to be cocooned Copley walked to his desk and picked up the phone; pushed the key for Scramble and waited. He gave the automated voice a code and waited again. Evelyn's voice eased his weary body and mind at any time. He needed to hear it now.

"Hello darling. Yes. All settled in. Exhausted. How did it go? Evelyn related the briefest of confirmation that the interview had taken place. No names. No location. "Settled in" meant Copley was at St James's. Copley was ready for bed. He exchanged the merest of thanks for the 'parcel' the information was much as he suspected. Pentland was the key. Why else would terrorists be in West Cumbria?

"I love you Evelyn."

Copley just relaxed into the words. His exterior was held together by the spit of venom; the glue of his life was Evelyn. He was a blob of nothing without. The reply came as an echo. With an instruction to get his head down.

Copley put the receiver down and headed for his bed. The crunch of boots on stone woke him. A sturdy remnant of the British Army protecting the monarchy acted as a good alarm clock. Within the hour Copley was comfortably ensconced in Simpsons with a trencherman breakfast before him and the company of his old and trusted friend Lord Gale.

Gale was something discreetly big in Whitehall. Copley was never quite sure what and never bothered to enquire. But. Importantly. He knew that Seymour Thwaites was not in the same pecking order of things. Thwaites was obviously oblivious of Copley's relationship with Gale, unless he dug very deep; on the surface they had no professional or political alliances. But what would one expect? Thwaites went to a Grammar school; no breeding; all pretension and no understanding of how things in Britain were truly run. Gale had been the chief instigator of Copley's introduction to the worldly delights of women in boots with a firm grip. Respect and honour was in the blood. However hard the like of Thwaites tried they would never have it. Copley's Mother was the descendant of two royal houses, but on the wrong side of the bed sheets. Copley had always considered this a good solid grounding; dynasties crumbled, mostly because they could not, or would not adapt. He was an adaption; all the right contacts without the straitjacket.

"What is it Copley? You ask me to breakfast and you hardly ever come to Simpsons because Evelyn says you need to watch your weight. You know she has spies everywhere. Come on. Spill the proverbial?

"Seymour Thwaites. He's gone rogue."

Gale looked Copley in the eye. Copley looked back.

"Why on earth would you say that. What evidence could you possibly have to make such an accusation? Thwaites is a highly experienced member of the MI6 directorate. Done a good deal of donkey work for HM over the years. Loyal. Trustworthy type."

"Because he's trying to hang me out to dry."

"Ahh. This body in the trench business. Bit dramatic I grant you. Coincidence. You digging? Where you are"

"I've been digging at Portsea for years. Nothing like this has happened before. Then we have the car crash and the fact it's not actually a crash but a very deliberate explosion. Somebody is piling on the theatricals and I think its Seymour."

"Why on earth would he do that?"

"Because Seymour is up to something, probably at Pentland and you are being kept in the dark."

"Something nuclear"

Copley watched Gale closely. Not a flicker.

"Pentland is our only reprocessing facility; creaking it maybe, but it is a triumph of British engineering. It's sensitive. Seymour would naturally be interested if there was a nuclear threat from terrorists. Its Seymour's job for heaven's sake."

"I don't doubt that there are terrorists, but I believe Seymour isn't coming clean with me. He's got my site crawling with anti-terrorism goons, expecting something, I know not what, to happen.

"You know better than most how it works. I grant you it all has landed on you, but I'm sure its coincidental, Copley. I assure you if there was anything, I'd tell you. Least as much as I could. But there isn't. Seymour is simply trying to catch some misguided fascists."

"Misguided! Dead body in my trench and a blown-up student. Misguided. Come off it George. "

"Nothing to do with Seymour. Just picking up the pieces. I know he will get your full cooperation"

"George it stinks; the source of this mess isn't a bunch of terrorists alone. Seymour is playing us for fools.

"Give me evidence"

"Erika Heinrich was working for us"

"Nonsense"

"Have it your way George. I leave it at that. You know my opinion. You should never let these grammar school types anywhere near the service; they get ideas."

It was a weak argument if true and Copley's last roll of the dice. More a lament than an argument. George was steadfast. The conversation turned to the sausages and how Cumberland should have protected status. Copley felt deflated. George wasn't having any of it.

George was sound. Perhaps Copley was wrong. No. He wasn't. there was no reason for Stumple to have left the note the way he did. He obviously wasn't taking any chances with surveillance. He'd probably twigged he was being recorded. He wanted to see Hamburg rather than the inside of a coffin.

It would be Copley and company versus Thwaites and the terrorists. Even odds thought Copley as he tucked into his egg. Nice and runny. Just the way he liked it. He would get Evelyn to make a few discreet enquiries with GSG 9, just to see how they reacted. The German and Austrian government would dearly like to see Britain brought to account over its nuclear policy; whilst they would never condone such barbarous acts the resultant mess it would offer a "Told you so" scenario that could easily alter British policy for the future. If there was a future. Would a nuclear bomb from the 1940's be viable and what was in the glass boxes? Was it something to do with the tiny capsule?

A direct attack on Pentland would be suicide. The more Copley thought, the more he contemplated the fact Thwaites knew far more than anyone about Pentland. How and why? Copley needed to find out and fast.

Determined not to spoil his breakfast he relaxed with thoughts of a few hours at Burlington House. Last place he'd find Thwaites. Good excuse for being in London. Use of the research library. He could sleep an afternoon away quite happily before catching a train North.

Copley sat at a wide screen monitor, gazing at a map on the one side of the screen and an aerial photograph on the other. The image was fine enough for Copley to work out specific features of structures. Pentland had once been a very large site indeed. The present facility encompassed less than a third of the wartime one. Could it be possible that the bomb was outside the perimeter? Forgotten? Surely that was utterly impossible. The British scientists would have taken it apart the moment they got hold of it. But a bomb, a nuclear bomb is just a series of components like any other. Copley was fully aware of the race for German technology from 1944 to the end of the war. Operation BIG and ALSOS had snatched technology from under the noses of the Soviets. The British had snatched technology from under the noses of both. It was no accident that Pentland became the home of the production of the British nuclear bomb. They had one to pay with courtesy of the Germans, But, why would a bunch of German fascists think they could locate a bomb without the British noticing and why wasn't Thwaites creating merry hell to stop it? George would have known; it would have filtered through. Thwaites was looking for terrorists. He knew damn well everything about them, He'd known every move with an agent in there all the time. Thwaites was playing a game. Copley was a side show. This was archaeology, Thwaites was having a bit of fun, buggering around with his dig and rubbing his face in it.

But where exactly were the remains of this bomb? Obviously not within the fence and how could anybody possibly have lost it? What was Thwaites going to do with it if he found it and what of the capsules?

Start with the landscape. Look and research. What is today is not what it was yesterday. Time changes all things, more than we care to think. We forget. Memory is transient. We record and it becomes dust in time. So much of the past has been deliberately hidden and forgotten. Chance being the best hope of rediscovery. Copley was going to have to change the odds.

Copley looked. He looked hard.

There were no shortages of photographs of the Pentland base during the second World War, some taken during the construction of various ammunition process structures; there was also a series of barracks, both for workers and workshops and ancillary buildings. Two buildings stood out to Copley. Two bungalows. They weren't on the 1939 ordnance, but there they were in 1944. Domestic looking bungalows. Copley knew camouflage well enough. Why go to the bother with so much in the way of military targets around them? The other odd factor was there was no road access to either; the only other genuine pre 1939 structure in the area had a clearly defined track to it. No. These buildings were odd. They were hiding something. Air filtration systems, which means a large underground facility, mused Copley. Bingo. Now to find the entrance.

Copley flicked through the available images, as he did, he noted the administration box on the image. It gave the date of when it had been last viewed. Six months ago. Interesting. Thought Copley. He checked a few more. All the same date. He opened the data box and the last user's identity. Seymour Thwaites. Copley smiled.

Not many people would want to look at these images unless they were doing the same as Copley and here was Seymour looking. Not getting a member of his staff. Personally, looking through them suggested Thwaites was playing a one-man game. Just instructing his team based on the head telling the body what to do. 'Cocky little sod Thwaites; you think you can win this one'. Copley muttered under his breath.

Copley expanded an image of a series of high explosive loading blast bank enclosures; these earth structures helped to prevent one mistake from turning into a total disaster, by containing an explosion. Copley scanned the structures. The angle was slightly oblique, creating shadow. To the left of the central blast bank a long deep shadow appeared to run along the outside edge of the bank, this shadow wasn't repeated anywhere else. There was a trench, an opening. Copley went to full magnification. There it was. There was even a pipeline heading into the void. No road, so a utility entrance. It gave Copley a line to work with. Give an archaeologist a straight line and they will look for a corner, an edge; from which they will deduce and enclosure. Copley noted the position, copied the image onto a modern map. It was way outside the present site line. It was utterly exposed, not just from a security perspective, but from the encroaching river estuary. Whatever was down there would be drowned in perhaps one more Winter or less. Copley worked his way North from the utility entrance. Nothing. He crept further North. Yes. Another long shadow; more pipes disappearing into the ground; a definite line. Copley tried another image, overlaid the data so far and tried Westward. A broad internal road heading for a building not much wider than the road itself. The road went no further. It just stopped at the building. Entrance.

From there Copley could plot two lines to intersect; two lines provide a corner and with the two utility entrances and the bungalows being within the square, Copley had the ground plan of the underground facility. He estimated it at about 48000 square metres; about eleven acres; impressive. Probably two storey; if other shadow factories were anything to go by. Copley was aware of this field of archaeology. These sites were popping up everywhere and costing millions to deal with. Copley knew there were no plans for any of them. Secret they were. This was by the far the biggest Copley had seen to date; it would have been built around 1937 onwards. By 1945 it would have been out of use the way the war was going and no Luftwaffe to worry about. An ideal location for a NAZI nuclear bomb, right next to a high explosives works. Typical British Army logic! In reality of course it actually made sense because of the chemists and scientists available and it's remote location if anything went wrong. Which was why the nuclear programme was sited there. Out of the way.

It had been a very big site in its day and now it was scrubby pasture, open to the rambler and any passing NAZI terrorist. The latest images showed nothing of any significance, the bungalows were gone. Gorse bushes and sheep were the only distinctive features.

Copley took the unprecedented step of copying his findings, bundling the whole into an email and sent it directly to George Gale. No accompanying note. George would know exactly whom, when and what. Sod protocol this was life or death for a lot of innocent people. There were times when the only course of action was to cut through the crap.

This was one of them.

George could work the rest out in the meantime whilst he caught up Copley was going to muster his troops and deal with Thwaites himself.

Copley walked out of Burlington House into a taxi, bound for Paddington.

At Paddington he boarded a train for Penzance. A meal and time to plan. Copley loved to sit in his comfortable seat, always the quiet coach, always facing the engine. He relished the ever-changing view. Britain was a wonderful country of contrast. Some lunatic was trying to mess with it and he wouldn't stand for that. Somebody was trying to mess with him. The steward delivered an early but much needed dinner, Copley chewed very slowly. Either Thwaites was a NAZI or he was using intelligence from his agent regarding the fascists for his own plot. He was of the opinion that Thwaites was after his own personal triumph. Was it enough to foil a potential terrorist plot? Hardly. That's what he was lavishly paid to do. Nobody would take notice of that. No. Thwaites was after the bomb, or part of it so he could get the upper hand at the highest level. He was trying to change the game. Which he had singularly not got over to George. The images and the access data should assist. Copley hoped rather than expected support.

What on earth could be down in that dark factory? He was aware that all sorts of things got forgotten about, the paperwork lost. Stored awaiting instructions. He had seen for himself railway carriages taken out of service and put to Ministry of War use that were still in the Big Four livery and in immaculate condition forty-five years after their withdrawal. All records of them destroyed. Still waiting in storage for orders for use that would never come. A bomb was slightly different, although he had heard a rumour that Pentland had for many years had a storage vault in which there was a dummy sea mine; only when after thirty years did they decide it was time to move it, that they found it was in fact still live and not a dummy. Had it not been for a sharp-eyed forklift driver, then a catastrophe would never have been averted. But an ultra-secret bomb. That was a completely different magnitude. Nobody lost one of those, No doubt the scientists from Germany would have been whisked away to work for us. There would have been plenty of people involved; plenty of equipment and laboratory staff. If Bletchley leaked its secrets like a sieve, why not this one? What was so significant. Was it that we kept it from the Americans, and they took exception? We built our own bomb to keep us in the race the German technology could have been vital. How many deaths to keep the German war machine going; how many postage stamps? Copley mused that it was a brilliant idea of the Germans to pay for their nuclear research by getting the German postage stamp to pay for it. Others paid with their lives by the thousands directly and millions indirectly. A dirty bomb. A very dirty bomb indeed.

Chapter Seven

Jessica took Jeff's hand, she turned to face him. She had never
felt embarrassed with eye contact. Jeff held her gaze, he was
by now feeling incredibly aroused. Jessica smiled; she
acknowledged his anticipation pulling him towards her still
holding his gaze as she slowly kissed his mouth.
Jeff kissed her back, he was passionate, hot for her.

Jessica pulled away gently.

" Slowly Jeff."

She led him over to a cushioned seat and sat him down;
kissing him all the while, she stood just in front of him as she
slowly undressed. Her blouse soft and silky hung beautifully
over her slim body, her breasts that completely bewitched Jeff,
were beautifully shown off under the material.
A lacy bra, thin and slightly see through showed enough of
her to indicate her now obvious arousal. She was ready for Jeff
The blouse now lay on the ground by her feet. Her skirt soon
joined it. Jeff was transfixed

"You're so beautiful Jessica"

She removed her bra and moving closer to Jeff she guided his
face towards her erect nipples. Jeff needed no encouragement
he was hungry for her. She moaned as Jeff licked and sucked
at her. He massaged her breasts and gently stroked her thighs
slipping one of his hands into her silky knickers. Gently his
fingers play with her cunt. She was moist, her lips opening
readily, low gasps filled the air as Jeff fingered her, her juices
easing his progression. Jessica was onto Jeff's trouser zip;
undone; his cock released, Jessica descended gracefully onto
her knees, gripping his cock in her right hand, guiding its
shaft expertly into her willing mouth.

Jeff's instinctively tipped his head back, his lips parted, breath quickening; offering himself whole to Jessica. He felt his balls being cupped and squeezed as she sucked him into her.

"God Jessica, I'm going to cum if you carry on much longer. I want to be inside you."

Jessica smiled

" You will be. Later. But now I want you to cum in my mouth. I want to taste you."

Jeff promptly obliged. The launch gently rocked. The sun shone down. Any intrepid climber would have had a bird's eye view of the lovers and no doubt wished them well. A cove, well away from the busy tourist launch circuit was an ideal spot, beneath the Watzmann; even the most earnest of tourist with binoculars would be looking up at the majestic mountain above. Jessica had come here often with her parents; now she was enjoying Jeff here. She drank him down. She felt him pump before he exploded into her mouth. She felt Jeff pump again, a final thrust, a final spurt. She drew him in. Deeper. She wanted all of him. She held him. He tasted of sweet earth, of light truffle straight from the ground. Passions fruit, a bounty of desire, a union of pleasure. Jeff had come a thousand miles further in his life journey in a matter of days. Life was good. Life was brilliant. Jessica. Satisfied and beaming lifted herself from the deck kissed Jeff deeply so he tasted himself and promptly took his now limp cock and waggled it.

"Come on. Much though I hate to say it. That (pointing at Jeff's cock) will have, to wait. We have a plane to catch."

Jessica eased the anchor free and the launch sped across the lake towards the village.

Back at Berchtesgaden Evelyn took a phone call from Ernie.

"Hello gorgeous. How's my favourite lady?"

"Ernie. What is it. Run out of pretty young students eager to get a First in fellatio?"

"One of the TV crew has just mentioned that they've had a tip off that there's to be a big anti-nuclear rally at Pentland."

"Thanks Ernie, that is useful. Any idea when?"

"Day after tomorrow. The police are being bussed in from all over and the site will be on lock down."

"How's it going with the goons?"

"To be honest they aren't a bother, bit of a rest for them. There's sod all going on here other than digging and if you hear from his lordship you can tell him, he was right, yet a bloody again. Some of the goons are pretty good in the trenches. This is turning out to be a huge waste of their time so far. But we wait and see. This demo. Might be something in it. Roads are open, but apparently, the nuclear site Police can stop and search anywhere. Everyone locally is used to this. I've seen it here before, never short of protestors here, especially when it's nice and sunny. But it might be significant what with …. What the fuck….."

The line went dead. Evelyn tried ringing back. Nothing. Not even a dial tone. Evelyn picked up another phone on her desk. Tapped a message into it and sent it.

AGRICOLA

Copley saw the text, it lifted him from his musing like a cold shower. He looked at his watch. Two more hours, then a taxi. Evelyn had organised the jet to Carlisle. That wouldn't really help unless he could get to Portsea quickly from there and that simply wasn't going to happen with the perilous state of the Cumbrian roads. He texted back.

WIPE

The reply.

ACK RED
Copley reached for his other phone.
A message appeared on the screen.

Ernie and students taken hostage. Copter at Barrow. Diverted jet acc. Backup on course.

Copley texted.

GEORGE Followed by. What the hell is going on?

Copley sat and wondered. The NAZI's had struck as Seymour has said. Seymour was right. He'd been barking up the wrong tree.

"Excuse me. Professor Copley? My phone. It's got a lady on it asking for you."

The gent at the opposite table handed over his phone, more than a little nonplussed.

"Copley. Listen. The goons have taken the students and Ernie hostage. They're working for Seymour Thwaites. He's turned his personnel. This whole NAZI Green Swastika is a pretense set up by Thwaites. I suspect they will be expecting you to head straight back. So don't, if they've infiltrated our network your jet won't make it, or the copter won't. Get off the train at Exeter. I will have a car waiting.
Love you take care."

Copley handed the phone back. Smiled at the gentleman whom still was wondering how the call had come through on his phone; but he shouldn't leave his Bluetooth on and the sophisticated gubbins in Copley's phone could drive the train should he want to, which he certainly did not.

Evelyn loved him. He liked it when she said it. It made everything alright when she did. It would be. Alright. He. They. Would sort it. The hostage taking was a side show, it would cause chaos and that was what Thwaites was looking for. Whilst it was evident that Thwaites would kill, or order persons to be killed, he was looking to get the maximum publicity facing at Portsea rather than at Pentland.

Copley looked at his address book, scrolling down and copying as he went. He tapped a contact.

"Hello Marjorie. Yes fine. I know. Horrific. I wasn't there. Terrible. Look. I want you to do something important for me; get the rambling club out to Pentland Wastes via the beach tomorrow. Ask Henry to have the master bring the pack out. I will sort the costs out. Yes. As many followers as possible. I will send details by text, or Evelyn will. This is extremely important. As many as you can. Yes. I will Thank You."

A plan was coming together.

Copley tapped a text.

ALL W I WC. Dir to follow

Sending it to Evelyn; he smiled. Thwaites wanted a fight. He was taking on the Women's Institute. He didn't stand a chance.

He understood that Ernie and the students were in a tight spot. But the heart of this was a rogue that was determined to gain personal power of some sort and kill a lot of people to do it. A few students and an archaeologist was nothing; he mused that the barman might not have made it to New Zealand, but hoped he had.

What was in that dark factory and what was the significance of the glass boxes and the capsule?

Copley contemplated. Yes. He was pompous. Yes. Aggressive and self-opinionated whenever he felt threatened; downright malicious when called for. Well this was a moment to put his skills to use, his ability to gain an audience's attention, to encourage; to discover. To unearth. He had no idea how he was going to get into that factory; obviously, Seymour Thwaites had found a way. Copley had some tricks up his sleeve. He had the locals; local knowledge, priceless in any campaign.

Copley tapped out a text, a round robin to every barman and landlord in the district, to discretely get some of the old boys together as soon as possible and find out what they knew of the secret factory. It would help regarding the hostage situation.

The BBC News had a distant blurred image of the excavation tents and Ernie being paraded outside the Finds Tent by one of the goons. The march on Pentland by the anti-nuclear brigade had been called off. The local anti-nuclear and national bodies were condemning the actions of the Green Swastika, whose demands for the closure of Pentland were all over the media. Nuclear spokespersons were making it up as they went along regarding the history of this terrorist group/ With good reason thought Copley. It was simply a front, or at least deluded individuals being persuaded by Thwaites. He suspected the MI6 officers involved to be completely under Thwaites spell. What was he peddling? A nuclear free Britain by any means, even if that meant massive loss of life. Why had he removed his agent? He had to, because she wasn't his agent. Erika was an MI6 officer, she must have realized that Thwaites had gone rogue, she must have told Kemp; Erika is killed and dumped for her girlfriend to find, she in turn attempts to get away. Somebody got to her car and restricted the traffic at the junction. Such takes organisation and planning. So, no doubt it was planned, in advance, to kill both women and do so at Portsea, deliberately in Copley's backyard. All the local attention and resources kept busy and away from the outskirts of Pentland, but with a perfect excuse to use Ministry resources in the area to hunt for terrorists' cells; even dig holes perhaps. Who would ask questions? Classic smoke and mirrors. Ernie and the students would have to endure. They would all be dead anyway if Thwaites or his cohorts got to the bomb, if bomb it still was. Somebody was confident that whatever was in that factory was a major game changer. There was only one way to find out. Get down there and use some of the enemy's tactics against them.

Copley stepped from the train. A car waiting for an extremely long road journey. Copley had thrown one of his phones under his seat on the train, just in case Thwaites was having him traced. Evelyn wasn't having him fly so she was taking the threat seriously. The car crawled out of the Penzance and into a supermarket car park; Copley was soon ensconced in an HGV watching the car leave with his other phone on board. He was going to retain the element of surprise as long as possible. He knew Thwaites would be waiting for him; part of this horror story was personal.

Chapter Eight

Copley was joined in the HGV by a British Army Intelligence Officer.

"Professor Copley you are to be transported to a secret location; from there, by helicopter, to Cumbria; courtesy of the Bundesnachrichtendienst and the Militärischer Abschirmdienst in a joint operation. For your benefit that's the German Federal intelligence and the military intelligence. The Germans are offering full cooperation as we have a bit of a problem knowing whose who on our side. We all need to stop this becoming an International incident. Just our luck theses chaps are down in the West Country on joint exercise. If Thwaites has a viable bomb it's potentially a global issue. The Germans will need to interview you on the helicopter. They have the tape and your additional information, but go through what happened again, anything could help. They obviously have some input as to what the NAZI's came up with. Stumple is doing the same in Stuttgart; he will be seeing a lot of German secure facilities until this is over. The RAF will escort you, so don't concern yourself with planes at your rotor tips.

Copley smiled. Dear old George Gale had got the message. Copley suspected he was already on the case, especially with the Germans so handy and willing to assist; but Copley knew he'd tipped the balance. All hell had broken loose, there had been arrests; political allies of Thwaites have been isolated. As for MI6. That would take a while to be sorted out. Thwaites has spun such a web a lot of loyal officers were just carrying out orders in the shady world of counter terrorisms unaware of the motive. Those with Ernie and the students were hardcore supporters of Thwaites. True motives unknown.

"Any questions? No. Right. Off you go driver"

Evelyn was addressing Jessica and Jeff; on the kitchen table Jeff could see a BBC Live view of the Portsea excavation. The tents looked insignificant; there were three students kneeling in front of the Mess tent with two of the goons standing over them with handguns. The sound was turned down, the picture changed to the Cumbrian Chief Constable, besides which stood Fremlins.

"That bastard works for Thwaites. He's one of them"

"Are you sure Jeff?"

"Yes. He was at the crash."

Evelyn calmly looked through her contact list, stepped away from the pair and waited for the phone to connect.

"George. Yes. I'm sorry but it appears that Fremlins could be implicated. Yes. Jeff saw him. At the crash site. Well I leave it to you. Yes. I know its developing by the moment. He's on the BBC News.

Jeff watched the screen. Fremlins moved away from the Chief Constable out of shot. There was some sort of commotion to the left of the Chief constable and the reporter. The camera followed the sound. Fremlins was being approached by two armed officers. He calmly took a gun from inside his left shoulder pocket; and before anyone could reach him, put it against his right ear and shot himself. The camera caught spatters of blood; the scene changed to the studio and a shocked news team.

"George. I'm sorry. Yes. Dreadful. Keep me informed. Copley. Goodness knows. I will let you know as soon as I know."

Evelyn looked at Jessica and Jeff. Jessica had never seen that look before. She tapped another number into her phone.

"You two don't have to come. We don't know if Seymour Thwaites has a viable bomb; if he does the consequences are unthinkable. I'm going because Copley's my life. I've put up with him. I've loved him; since the first time we met."

Jessica looked at Jeff. Jeff returned the same knowing look. Not a word was spoken.

Police sirens filled the air.

 "We better go down to the street. Our transport is here. Don't bother to pack. Just your passports"

Within minutes an unmarked car appeared outside the flat, accompanied by two Police cars. The convoy flashed its way out of Berchtesgaden.

Evelyn looked at her tablet. The international media were towing the line that this was an anti nuclear protest; not so widely known the head of MI6 had resigned and had promptly been detained along with her immediate senior officers. The breach in State security was being filled by MI9 and MI17 as per established protocols. The head of Civil Nuclear Security and Military Nuclear Intelligence were commanding operations covering an area from Glasgow to York. Civil authorities were being briefed.
The plight and immediate danger to the hostages was keeping the attention away from the greater threat.

As Jeff boarded the plane a headset had been thrust onto him and he had been briskly taken to the back of the plane. A link to a senior SAS commander required Jeff's personal knowledge of the students; layout of tents; how they were secured; any known health issues. The conversation was abrupt; urgent in the extreme.

Evelyn received a message from George Gale.

The Prime Minister had decided that an attempt would be made to free the hostages; likely on the morrow. Loss of life would, hopefully, be kept to a minimum.

Deadlines were being set. Yet Seymour Thwaites had kept silent.

Chapter Nine

Copley had thoroughly enjoyed his trip in the cab of an HGV, it gave one a whole new perspective on the World. He'd kept abreast of developments and heard from George Gale. That had boosted his morale no end. He was concerned for the students and Ernie, but they were a diversion. He suspected the goons had orders to hold out until Seymour was in a commanding position to give orders. It would be their only way out, being surrounded by highly trained marksmen and in the full knowledge of special forces. Keeping the hostages alive was the only chance for them.

Copley wondered how many personnel Seymour had at the factory site.   How easy was it to set a nuclear bomb off, or create a nuclear reaction? Of course, if Seymour was to benefit from the carnage he wouldn't want to be anywhere near when it happened. A fact not lost on George Gale.

George had objected to Copley's plan, but had tacitly agreed on the understanding that it was a subterfuge at some distance. That Copley was only to indicate where he thought Seymour and was and then to leave it to the specialists. No heroics. Evelyn would never forgive George if Copley was in the firing line.

The HGV came to a halt in a field. A helicopter, dimly lit was waiting. Copley boarded and was lifted aloft; high over the Severn and across the borderlands; high across Snowdonia. Ever present dots of light on either side; guiding angels pointed towards Cumbria. He used the time wisely. A Range Rover was waiting on his arrival; Copley dropped into its passenger seat. He had digested far too much information on nuclear bomb design in his long journey North. Casting his net wide for information on the factory site had born some results. Stories of tunnels with railway track; 'cave ins; suggesting that the site may well be in a perilous condition. One curious story told of a spot where radio signals were scrambled; only found by model plane enthusiasts with radio controls. This one spot scrambled the transmission causing the planes to be uncontrollable. Copley remembered that there had been jets over Portsea, something that was unusual because of the nuclear plant 'no fly' zone. Had Seymour been trying to pinpoint the spot? Within the hour Copley was sat with a pint before him, in his favourite Inn at Isdale; the bar was packed. A whiteboard had been propped up on the mantelpiece, a reasonable sketch of the Pentland Wastes had been drawn. The dunes to the West; the boundary of Pentland Nuclear to the North and the river to the South; the main railway line bordering to the East.

This was the sort of audience he enjoyed. Copley was in his element. These locals knew every inch of the terrain; it was a dialogue.

Two lads held their phones up acting as live feeds to other pubs; the landlord had a laptop camera facing Copley and whilst there was naught but a government crest to see on the screen a small red light indicated that the anonymous state was present as George Gale had insisted. Co-ordination was key. Copley was planning organised chaos.

As Copley had travelled across the County, he had considered the plight of Ernie in particular, If, any of the hostages was for the bullet it would be Ernie first because of his close relationship with Copley. This was personal. It was spite.

Copley's homework with the locals bore fruit. They assembled as he requested. Deep in the night a plan was revealed.

Copley thanked all for coming and explained in very frank terms the situation. That a rogue Government officer had accessed the abandoned underground facility on Pentland Wastes; that there was every chance that there was a device that could cause considerable risk to life and limb. That this individual had highly trained personnel protecting him. That the reason for the meeting was to set up a series of subterfuges to aid Special Forces to bring both the hostage at Portsea and at the factory site to a satisfactory end with minimum loss of life. That everyone, without exception, was to follow orders precisely and that military and other security personnel would be with each of the teams, at all times. Orders were to be followed without question; thousands of lives were at stake. Copley then stood up and moved to the map. Marker in hand.

"If the Beagle pack can make its way along the dune line from Cuthbert's Point traversing the land to the East in an arc towards the railway station and then back towards the North West that puts a high level of activity across the Waste with the minimum number of persons at risk. Followers can patrol the shore road to the station; effectively providing observers along the mile and a half stretch.

Ramblers. If you can proceed from the railway station across the Northern boundary along the old Pentland farm path. Keep to the footpath at all times; but take your time, nature watch, observe all the way. If the Mr Greggs and Mr Taylor are here? Your flocks will be loaded after this meeting, all the paperwork is in place. If you can release them when instructed from the goods yard and drive them onto the Waste. Mrs Coombes of the Women's Institute. If your ladies would accompany me on a field walk, meeting at the car park at the end of Shore Road. Bring as many ordnance maps doesn't matter of where, as you can. You will have company on your walk. Details will be texted to you. Please make sure you see the Police officers at the location you are viewing this; they need your details. I cannot stress how important it is you follow instructions. The Master of the Foxhounds please make yourself known to the officers who will join us after this meeting. Thank you for your assistance. Your efforts will undoubtedly make a significant difference. Please keep to the times and follow every instruction to the letter. We commence at seven sharp, but details of your exact times will be supplied. Thank You."

Copley wasn't taking questions and wasn't giving precise details; primarily because he didn't know exactly how Seymour Thwaites had got into the factory, what was in there, or what if anything he was going to do. In all this only the hostage takers had made demands and they had all been pretty run of the mill anti-nuclear stuff, except they were brandishing guns rather than banners.

Copley was in no mood to join the drinkers at the bar. Normally he would, but he had much to consider and he had mixed feelings about the arrival of Evelyn and even more about Jessica. What had Evelyn been thinking?

He took the back stairs up to his suite and noticed headlights beaming across the car park; doors opening and in the light he saw Evelyn and Jessica. Jeff followed. What had Copley got them all into too?

Copley had a gut feeling Thwaites was deliberately waiting for him, that this was all some mad vengeance, but for the life of him, Copley had all but no contact with the man, indeed his work was sound. If Copley said an archaeologist's work was sound it was normally ground-breaking and exceptional.

Copley heard footsteps and Evelyn and Jessica were on him like lions, with hugs. For all his concerns for their safety he was so glad to see them. He was aware Jeff was seeing another side of him, but no doubt Jeff had learned a lot in the last few days.

Jeff had been assigned the cottage, which was the property attached to the Inn. Jessica left Evelyn and Copley and slipped quietly way to the cottage with Jeff. Neither Copley nor Evelyn said a word.

"They seem well suited. Getting on well"

"Copley. Stop it. I see you have been busy. Any news of Ernie?"

"Food supplies have been taken in, one of the students with a medical condition has been released. Frankly I think they are playing for time. Thwaites has a timetable and they are working to it."

"I see you are trying some diversionary tactics of your own. George didn't seem to need much persuasion."

"George has got problems of his own, as you saw. As everyone saw. Fremlins. Bad business. What the hell is going on Evelyn. What possible motive; how on earth can there be a bomb down there that our lot didn't know about?"

"You are going to find out"

"Of course, I am"

"He could kill you. He could kill us all. This isn't our usual territory, we raise funds to dig, to teach; we influence, we deliver knowledge. We use knowledge at all level to drive research."

"The discovery of the unknown. Yes. That's what we do. No better example than this"

Evelyn looked at her phone.

"George has the LIDAR data for you. It will be quicker if we pop out to the car. There both fully equipped; George is providing everything he can."

They pair descended into the inky black darkness and the drivers stood to attention. Copley was aware there were other figures in the shadows. They sat in the back of one vehicle fitted with two large screens. Evelyn tapped in an access code and on the one the features of George Gale appeared. On the other a LIDAR image of Pentland Wastes.

"There you are Copley. Can you make sense of that? Our experts say it was a huge complex."

Copley studied the image and adjusted the angle.

"Yes. 48000 square feet. I estimate there's less than a third intact, if that; the reports I've heard speak of cave ins. How on earth there can be anything down there that is intact and viable after all these years beats me. By the way did you get the drones for me?"

"Twenty drones and pilots as requested, at your command"

"At your command. I suspect I won't be running the show once I get in there, if I can? What do the thermal images suggest in the way of goons?"

"Twenty above ground, they don't seem to move much, look if they are hidden from view; they are not intervening with the public heading for the shore."

"Below ground have you managed anything?"

"Not so easy but we have located activity in the Eastern sector. There appears to be power. It can only be fed from the main nuclear site. Pentland are trying to find he actual source and sever it."

"Not sure that's a good idea, we don't know what state or what process is going on; it might also get Ernie killed or worse. Thwaites has his bargaining chips nicely set up."

The image of Gale started speaking and the voice on the loudspeaker tried to catch up.

"Copley. I'm going along with this because, frankly the Prime Minister says I should let you; your role is to divert, not intervene. If you can find a viable entrance, then it's our teams that go in. Not you. You can keep the goons busy, but we do the hard part. Understood."

"Absolutely George. Loud and clear"

"Good. That's settled. I'm still not happy that Evelyn and Jessica are there, but you are the luckiest man alive Copley to have Evelyn as a partner. If you get out of this alive, I'm going to insist you two get married or I shall have you both arrested. You hear me. Both. Now get some rest. Goodnight Evelyn."

"Goodnight George"

Copley looked at Evelyn, held her hand and kissed her. Deep longingly. Copley simply didn't do that in public. But things were very different. This wasn't normal. Evelyn held him close and for a moment the stars shone brighter over Isdale as they embraced. Copley held Evelyn tight; he didn't ever want to let her go. The ever, diplomatic driver opened the door and the shadows discreetly moved back as the pair walked back into the Inn.

Copley was going to make love to Evelyn. It may be his last time. Oh no. Copley was made of sterner stuff than that. He closed the door of their suite. A security officer positioned himself in front of it. Jessica smiled at Jeff as she shut the front door. The cottage was warm and cosy, although a little dark inside, it had a welcoming feel about it. Jeff took her hand and started to pull her towards the stairs, keen to continue his sexual exploration of this beautiful and exciting woman. But Jessica, who definitely wanted to continue their sexual delights, pulled Jeff in a different direction.

"Let's find the kitchen"

Jeff a little disappointed duly followed.

Along the hallway and straight-ahead Jessica found the most important room of any home.

As she had hoped, a large solid wooden table stood in the middle of the kitchen, with half a dozen or so study wooden chairs around it. Jeff still feeling a little disappointed offered to make tea. Turning to Jessica to ask how she liked it Jeff's face changed from hard done by little boy to cat that had the cream. Jessica had slipped her dress and knickers off and was sitting on the kitchen table. She undid her bra and threw it onto the pile of discarded clothes. Teasingly she cupped both her breasts and started to massage them. Jeff bewitched stood and watched as Jessica slowly turned herself on. Holding both nipples between her thumb and forefinger she pulled and twisted them. Her eyes were sparkling with mischief and her nipples red and very pert. She moved her right hand slowly down and opened her legs wide enough for Jeff to see her now moist cunt. With her right hand she stoked her clit and lips, moving two fingers inside her cunt. She held Jeff's gaze; his erection now very visible. He moved slowly towards her, his mouth open and eyes full of desire and excitement Jessica offered her fingers to Jeff's mouth. He delighted in the taste of her and moved in closer to kiss her mouth. Jeff was on fire. His cock strained hard against the material of his trousers and a small telling damp patch had appeared. Jessica had moved closer to the edge of the table and leaned back, her arms supporting her. Jeff sucking her nipples moved his mouth down towards her belly. He sat down on one of the wooden chairs and moved his mouth towards the inside of Jessica's thighs. She shivered with expectation and as Jeff started to kiss and probe her cunt with his tongue she dropped her head back and her breathing now quickened. Jeff stood up and kissed Jessica deeply His tongue explored her mouth passionately, his hands cupped both breasts, massaging them; fingers squeezing her nipples. All the while his mouth explored. Jessica; passion ignited, moved Jeff's hands down to her cunt. Jeff slowly fingered her. Rubbing her clit with his thumb, now moist with Jessica's juices.

Jessica, tongue deep inside Jeff's mouth, breathing fast, urgent, to breathless by Jeff's fingers moving faster, in and out flicking and stroking her cunt, Jessica thrust her body hard onto Jeff's hand Jeff felt her cunt grip his wet fingers. Knowing a climax approached Jeff was beyond just being aroused; beyond lust, a connection, a union of desire, a fascination. Jeff watched Jessica as she climaxed, felt her whole-body shiver and shudder, his fingers still pushed deep inside her; his thumb firmly stroked her clit. Jeff was amazed at Jessica's ability to ride her orgasm. Jessica gazed into Jeff's eyes; smiling and with great purpose she undid his trousers

" Right darling, I think we're both ready for a good fuck now."

Jeff pulled his trousers down and kicked them off Jessica laughed as she helped pull down his damp boxers, Jeff looked into her eyes, full of desire and admiration. His cock hard, his legs trembling as he eased himself into her; groaning with pleasure as he pushed his cock deep inside her as she laid herself back down onto the table, her eyes shut her mouth open, her body rippling in time with Jeff's thrust. He gripped her thighs as he pushed his cock deeper still into her cunt. Jessica propped herself up to watch her lovers progress Jeff smiled at her, he was so close he can feel he is at the point of no return. Jessica felt his cock relax inside her and then shudder, as it pumped hot spunk into her cunt. Jeff cried out and gripped her thighs still thrusting into her.
Jeff was done, his legs nearly gave way. He laughed as Jessica wrapped her arms around him and drew him in for a kiss.

"Bloody hell, that was good."

Jeff helped Jessica down from the table.

"I really fancy that cuppa now" he winked.

"Tea and bed, Mummy was quiet on the plane. I know there was a lot of messages; but I suspect it's going to be a tough day. Looked grim at Portsea. "

Jeff was still pulling himself together, the sex had cleared his head, he felt revived; the reality of the situation hit home. Jessica boiled a kettle; there were some biscuits, a tray and a staircase to a comfortable double bed. Whatever happened he was with Jessica and with Evelyn and Copley about, it would be sorted.

"It will be ok, Jessica. Your parents can sort anything"

"Daddy doesn't normally get involved with anything as dangerous as this.; least I don't think he has. Most of the time it's a case of somebody knowing somebody that can fund or support a project; or get something done. They're both masters of persuasion."

"Copley"

"Yes. He can be. You don't know him yet. Anyway, let's get up those stairs. Early start no doubt. Come on."

The pair turned the light off on the kitchen and headed for the first-floor bedroom. Outside the security officer radioed their movement into control. Up in the bedroom Jeff and Jessica lay in each other's arms. Their first experience of lying next to each other in a bed. Which is exactly how they were when Jeff became aware there was someone in the room with them. He'd woken with a start; on his guard.

"Stay still, don't put the light on."

"Evelyn"

"Wake Jessica, keep her quiet."

Jeff duly shook Jessica who responded by trying to embrace him.

"Jessica, your Mothers here. Keep quiet. Somethings going on."

"What? Mummy? What is it?

"I've had a message from German Intelligence. We need to get out of here. Grab your clothes and coat, keep it quiet' they are watching the cottage. Your Father's fast asleep; I need you out of here, without anyone seeing you"

"They're watching us. How can we get out?"

"This cottage and the Inn are connected by servant passageways; the Inn is riddled with secret rooms and tunnels. That's why we come here. Now get your act together and keep it quiet"

Within five minutes the three were ready and standing on the landing. Evelyn opened the lid of the window seat, the front unbolted offering a wide enough access point to a ladder. In the ancient gloom; they descended; bolting and dropping the lid behind them. Security outside being none the wiser.

Chapter Eleven

The sun shone over the Pentland Waste. A couple of beagles sniffed amongst the dunes; followed by another; the hunt was on the move. A small band of hikers were leaving the station car park heading for the coast. Another party of long-distance walkers with large backpacks were heading up toward the station. A minibus wandered down the shore road. Stopped and a group of ladies decanted with a gentleman leading them, using his hat as a pointer to various features of the landscape. The wastes were alive with people. A flock of sheep was being released into the mix; Anyone observing the scene would have their work cut out to identify any one group or individual of note. The sheep were conveniently, from Copley's perspective standing in the way of anyone trying to use binoculars and would shortly, along with the beagles start to flush out the goons. A solitary drone, operated by a child in the shore car park wandered along the shore road, away from the site, but gaining height provide a bird's eye view of the operation. The Wastes were a veritable Piccadilly Circus. Some of the backpackers had stopped for a drink. The hunt was working its way into the scrub and gorse. The second flock of sheep had been released and were being driven by sheep dogs directly towards the site. The ramblers had strung themselves out with some taking a very leisurely pace at the rear. One or two of the ladies with the man in the hat had popped behind a gorse bush. Three drones rose from the beach and hovered high above the site. Another three followed; the furthest to the east faltered and fell from the sky. Another approached on a southerly trajectory and likewise fell. Another three rose and held clear of an inviable line in the sky. At the same time there was a rustling in the gorse. Any bystander would have noticed the backpackers had lost five members; the walker likewise, the hunt had likewise five less followers, the ladies had not come back from their call of nature. The man with the hat had vanished.

Seymour Thwaites forces above ground were neutralized. His communications broken by drones identifying the frequencies and jamming them. Twenty men captured alive for questioning without a shot being fired. All Copley now had to do was locate the entrance and to do that the downed drones gave him a position for the strange jammer beneath the earth. Somewhere close by must be the entrance. Copley had thoroughly enjoyed the diversions. It had kept the goons extremely busy and the amount of radio traffic had provided the frequency and the locations necessary to take all of them out. There was no doubt Seymour Thwaites was trapped, but Copley also knew that whatever he had control of was powerful enough to be a bargaining tool. One man against a country. It had to be big and very dangerous.

"Well that went smoothly enough; now to winkle him out. Thank you, Professor"

The Special Forces Officer stood surveying the line of goons being marched to waiting transport. The Hunt passed them in the same direction their quarry found they had one more mission to perform. Copley smiled to himself.

"Now to winkle him out. Got a big pin handy?"

"We'll take it from here. We have our orders."

"Yes. George doesn't want me down there, but he would like me to help, to find how to get there. Seems a little unfair considering what we've just achieved don't you think?"

"Orders. You know how it works"

"Orders. Ahh yes. Orders. Following orders. I'm an archaeologist, not a military man. We have much in common; you can read a landscape, the terrain, the soil types. Dust. Mud. Vegetation types and patterns. But you lack the vital spark, that ability to work that information backwards, to imagine and to ask the why, build the worlds and break them down again, repeat it, build high, or low. Palaces, ruins, farmstead to factory all within three inches of us. You read the present, I read the past. That past that made the now. Archaeologists. What are we? We dig the rubbish of the past, we sieve the detritus and we make pretty patterns, we invent with the fragments, like children playing in the sand. Our constructs give insight. The stand and fall as our reputations ebb and flow. We remind humankind that all is but dust; that how we got to our place is as fragile as our breath to our being; we are necessary, without it we are but grey forgotten things without worth."

"You're still not going down that hole"

"Ahh. You saw it too. I confess I didn't think you had"

A large gorse bush next to Copley and the officer showed recent signs of being in contact with a jacket, the material was at the very bottom branches, suggesting someone had crawled out or in; from the disturbance of the grass there was dry dead gorse on fresh green sod, suggesting it was recent egress. One of the goons had been drawn out probably by the general activity. The gorse canopy wasn't that thick and a small patch of red, red oxide could just be seen. A hatch cover in the open position. Both Copley and the officer had seen it at just about the same moment and had strode towards it and each other without trying to attract to much attention.

"You are not going down there. I have my orders!

"I'm afraid your orders have nothing to do with me "

Copley raised his left arm which distracted the officer at the same time Copley jabbed a hypodermic in his right hand into the officer's neck.

"Sorry about that but I need to have a chat with Seymour Thwaites"

The officer went to retaliate and with a look of utter confusion and no little embarrassment at being outwitted by a rotund middle-aged archaeologist, sagged to his knees and fell flat on his face. Copley neatly put him in the recovery position and headed for the hatch. Amazing what archaeologist can keep in their pockets. Copley had more than once considered using that hypodermic on one of his more truculent post-graduates. He'd got it from a vet pal of his down the pub. Knock a horse out. How long ago was that? Well he looked a pretty healthy chap. No harm done. Soon sleep it off.

"Here we go Copley. Seymour Thwaites here I come."

Copley lowered himself onto the metal rungs and descended the narrow shaft into the depths. He counted the rungs, thirty. Not that deep. The air was clean and warm, better than he had expected, and a gloomy light revealed a white painted corridor. Concrete and steel for the most part; a typical secret factory construction; functional. Copley knew he was at a service hatch associated with the now long-gone steam pipework that had run at service level before diving into the depths. Large steel doors to his right indicated their remains. There was a distant hum, no sound of movement. Copley looked for a camera near the hatch. There was none, nor had he seen anything on the surface. Seymour's attitude towards security, his perimeter certainly, was frankly tardy. Deliberately so, thought Copley. Because he really didn't have to bother. Just enough time to draw attention to his demands; the student hostages; the body in the trench, the explosion. Even the jets trying to locate a radio anomaly. It was all a signpost. What sort of man leaves himself undefended and vulnerable. One that knows he is completely safe whatever is thrown at him.

Copley walked slowly down the corridor to the left, following the humming. Gloomy bulb after gloomy bulb, six bulbs later his path was blocked by timber and a vast mound of concrete. Poured concrete that had broken its shuttering. The corridor was filled to the roof. Just poured in, flowing out like a blancmange; sign of desperation, a sign that something very serious had happened beyond and the way had to be blocked very quickly indeed. Copley looked at the concrete. There was material in it. There was bone. For once Copley shuddered. He simply didn't shudder. He had kissed the dead before. But there was something very wrong about what he was seeing. It made him want to run. Without hesitation he turned. He wanted to get away from that sight as quickly as he could; passing the hatch where he'd entered; there was more urgency in his step, as if he was being followed. A terror swept over him, ran in front of him. Looked him in the face. It passed leaving him a sick feeling in his gut.   Out of the gloom he could see a figure standing at the end of the corridor.

"Copley"
"Seymour fucking Thwaites"
"Really. Copley, descending to the language of the herd"
"What the hell are you doing Thwaites You know you are surrounded and by the way I take it very personally that you have taken my students and Ernie hostage?"
"But my dear Copley, you have worked out that I'm not in the least bit concerned. In fact you could shoot me now and it would make not a jot of difference. I've won."
Copley walked up to Thwaites. In the gloom his face was a series of craggy lines with a ghastly smile sticking out of it.
"Let my students go"

"I have absolutely no interest in your students. No doubt you will be trying the same tactics at Portsea as you did here. I must admit I was amused at your antics. You will get your students back and Ernie; much good it will do any of you. Ohh why does that man put up with you. Perfectly decent excavation director and he ends up working for you. Just like Evelyn. Wonderful woman, stuck with you. Nailed to your cross. Well it doesn't matter now. Nothing matters now. Come on Copley. I think as I put your excavation to such good use you deserve to see this."

A door off the corridor opened into a large anti chamber, a changing room at the end which was as set of glass panelled doors.

Seymour sat on one of the benches and looked up at the standing Copley. Seymour casually looked at his watch. Copley just gazed at him.

"I've nothing much to say Copley, certainly no defenses, other than I regret nothing. As for motive, think what you like. Truth is what you make it. I could hold Europe to ransom with what is behind those doors. I was going to do just that. You will, I hope, allow me to suggest I was always thorough with my archaeological research; I had a passion for going over ground again, seeing what others had missed. I always had an eye for the ephemera of finds, the oddity, the loose end and the relationships that were naught but mere shadows; but combined with thorough forensic investigation made for a clear pattern, routes to the forgotten. Just as your own work occasionally flowers, if you only looked beyond your own pomposity. Too late, now, I fear.

I sit here content. I discovered the forgotten, it's what we do. What I did, when archaeology filled my head, That, seems several lifetimes ago. How a nation a can lose thirty nuclear bombs? Anything is possible with this decrepit country; ashamed of it's true past, incapable of accepting its fallen self. Burying what it can't cope with. After the accident, the order was given to seal off all the bombs; but all that happened was the sites were sealed. The bombs were supposed to be monitored but the level of secrecy was such that the orders never reached the workface. Nobody was supposed to know these bombs existed. Certainly, not the Americans or Russians. The truth, the farcical truth is they were lost. All these years. Lying forgotten; waiting. The ultimate weapon Copley, the nemesis of an entire nation. Waiting its moment. Seems a far cry from archaeology, but Copley we choose our path and I was ambitious for power. You took the academic path, I took the political route; Royal commissions; a smiling affable committee man; nodding at the right time, making the ministerial contacts. Slowly, inevitably I ended up working in MI6; because I was deemed as the thorough researcher. I could sit and quietly laugh at these shadowy departments and their mandarins, to me they were just the knuckledusters of a tired regime and I decided I would subvert them, to my own end. Because I could. They were fools. Like you Copley. They have a belief in the order of things; the swan continues to glide and doesn't even wonder how it does so. You and I know its drowning, just we pretend all is normal. Well I stopped pretending.

The more I witnessed the level of rot, the fatuous belief that Britain could continue to claim a seat at the top table of nations: the more I decided to put it firmly and irrevocably in its place. To burst the bubble; that holier than thou, myth of greatness. It's all gone. Faded away, save in the mind. A nation that harks back constantly to the Second World War; the last great victory, seventy years ago. Because it has nothing left. Refusing to accept reality, still telling everyone what to do; empty barrels, hollow ships and indignation. Not a country at all. A petty disgrace interfering where it has no justifiable right. With its moral indignation and self-importance transparent to all; orders as if it has mighty forces to deploy. Spent. Farcical. Punching above its weight. Well somebody is going to punch back. Me. I decided to put it out of its misery. Either take control, to force the Government to face the reality, or simply to destroy the whole sorry mess. I confess I was of an open mind. For a moment. From ashes great nations rise. Germany is great again; It was to fall to rise, stronger, invincible. A slate wiped clean Yes. How glorious to see Britain in ashes, the let time and history play its part. A new order, clean, untarnished by hypocrisy. Perhaps the name will change? A new land, needs a new order. Anything is better than this. Let it perish."

"Prey tell me where do people like you fit into this great new order? Not the leader of the Green Swastika. I mean, if you have your way, we are going to die, if I'm not mistaken. Not that any of this makes much sense other than you are sick in the head and probably always were. Thwaites not your real surname, is it? Schneider. That aside, I grant you had some influence and power in MI6, but I don't believe you had that level of authority to subvert as much as you have. So. With absolute certainty I suggest I'm talking to the monkey not the organ grinder. A pretty sick monkey too. Swallowed a whole bucket of hate of us. You don't understand the British, we are a very unusual breed. We envelop extremism with afternoon tea and decency; we play our part in the World through respect, not the size of our guns. We have a Union flag not a Swastika.

"Copley. It's only a name; you've seen the rise of the far right across Europe. Names, groups. One idea. Oh, they wave their flags and want to expel everyone that doesn't agree with their view. There I see the point. They want to wipe away all that does not belong. Restorative change; removing the canker to allow fresh life to grow, a cut deep into the jugular and to me the fascists were a means to an end. Without the far right I would never have found the bombs. I used our intelligence network, infiltrated and syphoned off what I needed to know. You see Copley. I don't matter, you and I know we are history; all our works will be forgotten. If you are lucky something of the great Copley may survive the ravages of time. Archaeologists and historians may have you as a footnote, an obscure echo from another age. But. I will be remembered forever. The man that levelled the playing field, let Europe breathe again; wiped the annoying British out of the game for once and for all. Once I realized to what lengths the British would stoop to keep Europe fractured to suit its own plans, I decided I would use my position to find a means of destroying the whole rotten island."

"One bomb won't do that Thwaites. It will make a mess, but we are used to them. We get by, we come through. You know that. You poor deluded man, you think we are frightened of you."

"One bomb. You know nothing. One bomb. Ha. Fool. The British didn't take a bomb from Berchtesgaden, they took thirty. Yes thirty. Right from under the noses of the Americans. Why do you think the Americans have kept a special relationship with you? You had the bomb before anybody; we let you have it; how else do you think it was quietly vanished away. The British viewed it as a great success, a bargaining chip. German High Command was thinking far ahead; knowing the end was nigh, that Germany would gain American aid to fend off the Russians. Germany by its efforts would rise again; whereas Britain would wither, become a quagmire of its own making, let's face it Copley, this country has decayed around us. America has always been suspicious of the British. They have always suspected we had a hidden weapon and when we unveiled our own bomb, the suspicion grew stronger, The German high Command knew it would create a deep rift. The bombs were more deadly not exploding. From that moment on Britain entered a twilight world and has never quite understood what went so wrong. "

Seymour looked at his watch again. Copley stayed stone faced.

"Nothing you've said Seymour makes me believe you are anything but a pathetic misguided wretch. Your mewing about our perilous state; you can hear that in any pub after six pints. I grant you the number of bombs is surprising considering the scale of the process need to make them. It may well explain the deficiencies in the German war effort, if such vast amounts were being spent on this technology, but this is over seventy years ago; none of it will possibly be viable."

"I thought that. I had heard rumours of the German bomb; how the Germans were approaching the whole process from the wrong angle' then I saw through some of the disinformation, did my own digging, literally. Went to the bars and listened. It's what we do isn't it? We listen, we observe, we see where others have no perception. They, our Lords and masters, live in blissful ignorance. We see, we delve; disturb and become part of the past. I found the facility. It was truly amazing. The effort, the sheer scale."

"The slave labour"

"You a Romanist objecting to slaves. Ha. That's a good one" Seymour glanced at his watch again.

"I will have to be going now. I wish I had time to try to convince you of my reasoning. I just hate this country and all it has become"

"Twaddle. Sheer twaddle, Your raving Seymour. Who's really behind this?"

"Twaddle. I suppose to you it is, I don't really care. I had dreams once, I had power for myself. Now? I don't matter. All is dust. On that Copley we must agree? My grand designs are not for me to see, I can only imagine; that's what we do Copley. You have your dirty little past Copley. Remember some of us know about the Agricola project. Some of us know how the sinews of fact are stretched thin, especially by you; your visions of the Roman age. I nearly sympathise. We dream and hope that the earth gives us the clues that we knit our world together with. Our Worlds. At least my world will become a reality. Britain, a desert; reduced to begging for relief; dispersed. The delightful part is that you brought it upon yourself. Your final destruction. You took the bait. We played the long game. I'm merely the last in a line of messengers, slowly working our way into your nest; each picking up a piece of the puzzle and turning the page until all is finally revealed. All I had to do was flick the switch. As for you Copley. I knew there was a site close to your dig. I'm sorry couldn't help myself; a final dig at Copley. Not to be missed. A grammar schoolboy getting the better of you. Never. Not possible. Oh. I know what you think of me, my sort. The lower orders. We don't belong. The establishment has a place for us. We can rise but we must remember our betters. We all know where you came from. Ironic it being a German bomb."

"I suppose you couldn't help yourself when you killed Erika, Hanna and all those at the junction."

"If you had time you could ask George Gale where all those bodies came from. I just borrowed them. Erika. She was working for me and for George; pity for her I found out. Unfortunate. Like this whole business. If only the British hadn't decided to get in our way so often. I really do begin to understand how Napoleon felt."

Seymour stood up. Smiled at Copley and proceeded towards the double door. Copley grabbed at his arm. Seymour turned. Looked at Copley.

"Sorry Copley the games up for you, up for all of you. I suppose you might as well come and see. It makes no difference now."

Seymour pushed the doors open. Copley followed and stopped in his tracks.

A large well-lit room dominated by a cream coloured metal box the size of a car. Pipes ran to it from out of the floor. A second smaller box the size of an old television sat on a pedestal a short distance away, narrow metal tracks ran between the two. On the wall was a large metal dial with wires coming from a series of stations. In the stations were small glass boxes. These must be the glass boxes described by Stumple thought Copley.

"There were two bombs here originally. In 1945 they tried to disassemble it. You saw the result down the corridor. The Germans didn't just send a bomb; they sent a nerve agent, triggered when the bomb was tampered with; the factory personnel went mad; the authorities buried them alive. They shot any trying to escape. Shot them like dogs and concreted over their mistake. You felt an overwhelming feel of terror near that concrete? It's still active. Which is why Erika and the personnel that helped me were fitted with a nasal filter which counteracted the nerve agent. Simple and effective, but obvious if I'd left it in her body. Although I have to admit I feel different than I did at first. I'm no longer bothered about why I'm going to kill you all. I have become death, just for the sake of it. I do hate you all. But I mustn't spoil the tour. You see that small box, which you may gather is heading towards the big one. Looks like an ice cream maker to me. Well it only has to get within about nine inches of the other one and Nothing. Oblivion. All gone. Not just here twenty-eight other sites. All gone. Allowing for Pentland next door, that's complete annihilation, with the other sites all next to nuclear facilities, complete eradication. No more Britain. Each one of those boxes represent a bomb, all connected to this one. When the first bomb proved so difficult to handle, they were dispersed, and a monitoring system installed. I just reconnected it and with the manual I just turned the mechanisms back on. The Germans hadn't developed a delivery system, but that's no problem when you are detonating it on the spot. More a case of understanding mechanics of getting those cogs to work. Bit of grease and a wrench, hardly physics. All the circuits and chemicals absolutely as sound as they were seventy years ago. German engineering at its best. "

I admit it's not what I expected. I don't doubt for one moment it will work, but why is it I don't feel any effects as I did down the corridor?"

"We deactivated the tamper safe device"

"So why are you …"

Seymour fell to the floor.

"Ahh. Well I can answer the question, the filter only works for so long; we found it eventually causes neurological damage and ….

"Kills you"

Seymour slipped away from Copley. Death was smiling up at him with a sickly grin and spume. Copley stared back. Seymour's features were distorting. His sinus was expanding. Blood poured from his nose followed by what appeared to be brain tissue. Copley recoiled. Brought to his senses by the small cart moving ever closer to the big one. Seymour had held out just long enough to distract his attention. The cart was approaching a chalk mark on the floor. Seymour had estimated the distance before annihilation. Copley ran to the machine and put his weight against it. No avail. It was still moving. Beads of sweat appeared. Fear and exertion. Evelyn and Jessica appeared in his mind. No. He wasn't going to see them die. He was an archaeologist and you don't mess with archaeologists. They don't give in. He reached into his coat pocket. Grabbed his trusty trowel and with a micro moment of regret thrust it into the heavy gearing of the wheel mechanism. The cart jolted. It jolted again. The white line was within a paper width distance. The cart stopped; the cogs ground themselves, groaned, squealed and then there was a sharp pistol like snap. The trowel had done its job, the cog wheel flew across the room and hit one of the glass boxes. Copley could see a crack appearing and a fluid oozing out. The fluid gone it revealed a word in the back of the container "UNSCHARF". Seeing the cart was disabled and the word appear he recognized that the glass containers were some form of pressure driven trigger mechanism, to go off in sequence as the Pentland bomb exploded.

At that moment three special forces personnel entered the room.

Copley yelled at them.

"For fuck sake shoot those glass boxes."

Without another word the entire panel was a sea of glass splinters, liquid was oozing out of the containers. Copley reckoned it wasn't going to be gin and tonic and wasn't going to wait to find out. One of the officer's hand him a respirator and they were about to retreat when Copley pointed to the small box. Indicating it had to be taken with them. Copley took the opportunity to rescue his trowel. Forged Sheffield steel, nothing quite like it, a proper trowel. An archaeologist should never be without one, this was a case in point. Between the four of them they lifted the box off the rail and through into the changing room where Copley signed to drop it and run. Behind them a screeching sound emanated from the small box and a beam of light pierced the wall. A shine path, suspected Copley, an immediate need to escape overtook him. They could hear the panel explode in a crescendo of cascading glass, the air was thick with smoke and sweaty terror. It was a race to the hatch with fear chasing all of them. A climb that seemed to last forever. At last. The sky. Quite a party was waiting for them, all looking non-human, anti-contamination suits. The four were bundled away as pipes were thrust into the hatch way and expanding foam was poured in to prevent anything from escaping. Copley was manhandled, his clothes cut from his body and he was dragged into a decontamination shower and scrubbed until it felt as if his skin would come off. Eventually he was handed towels; his body was monitored with a portable Geiger counter and swabs were taken from his mouth, nose and arse. Dressed in a paper suit he was frog marched to a portacabin that had appeared in the relatively short time he had been below ground.

"Copley"

"George"

"Copley. Do you ever follow orders?"

"Is he alright? That Special Forces chap."

"Bruised pride, I think. He should have known better with you.

"Ernie and the students, are they alright?"

"Yes. The ruse with the beagles worked. Those foxhounds, too; they just go through anything especially with a drone laying down a scent. All tidied up. No students injured. Ernie took a bit of a pasting, but nothing that he hasn't suffered on a Saturday night.

Now. Seymour Thwaites, did he tell you why he did this? Who was he working for?"

"That's the odd bit George, he seems to have done this all off his own back; he wasn't the arrogant Thwaites that I saw at Isel Hall. He was rambling towards the end. The nerve agent suppressant eventually killed him. I suspect there was limited supplies of the stuff, he held onto the last. Pathetic really. Rambling. Sorry mess."

"Copley the country owes you a debt of thanks. The Prime Minister would like to talk to you. She will meet you at the Inn in forty minutes."

"Can I have some clothes and where's my watch and trowel?

"Being checked for contamination. I will get them to you with a change of clothes. Copley. Thank you. You really are going to be unbearable after this…"
"George. I won't change a bit"
"That's what worries me."

George departed. Chance for Copley to catch his breath, the scrub down had invigorated him. His head was clear of the terrors, the drug had a lasting effect, Thank goodness. Copley suddenly realised that he hadn't been debriefed, that nobody knew of the anti-tamper and the nerve gas. The special forces chaps wore that sort of gear and they had been prepared to rescue him and of course they may have been carrying gas themselves, but the bombs everywhere else. If anyone went near? Copley stepped out of the portacabin straight into a special forces officer.

"I've not told anyone that the other bombs have anti-tamper features"

"No problem sir, we know"

Copley stepped back inside.

"How did they know" He said out loud. Something wasn't quite right here. Seymour has said something about borrowing bodies from George Gale. No phone, he couldn't ring Evelyn. He was naked.

The door opened and a military policeman dropped in a pair of trousers, socks, shirt and black boots. Copley looked like a scruffy policeman, but he at least had clothes. A dark blue jumper finished the ensemble. His watch and trowel were in a plastic bag. Hardly how he would like to meet the PM, but at least he would see Evelyn.

Within ten minutes Copley was sat in the passenger seat of a Land Rover heading for Isdale. The driver said not a word; Copley was use to diplomatic silences; he looked at his watch, just enough time to put a suit on before the meeting with the PM. Isdale swung into view, the glorious dale of the Western Fells and the Isdale Inn.

Duly deposited he ran up the stairs to his room like a teenager. His boots thumping on the stairs. Odd thought Copley. Evelyn must be on the phone. He entered the room. Nobody. Of course she would be with Jeff and Jessica at Portsea. Foolish of him, he all but ripped the police clothes from his back and went to the wardrobe. Finding a shirt and suit, he changed in double quick time. Odd he thought, where was his spare mobile and laptop? Copley stopped in mid tie; he just felt something was wrong. The car park was remarkably empty and the bar unusually quiet. Cleared he thought, because of the PM. No. Something wasn't right. He had seen police stationed outside. Seymour's comment about George came back to him.

Copley went downstairs with an air of a man that has just stopped a nuclear catastrophe, relief all over his face; but with a hidden dread that it was a hollow victory and an old friend had questions to answer. Copley would bluff it through. It could just be a reaction to the traces of nerve agent. No. he really did believe George had questions to answer.

The bar was empty. Silent. Copley poured himself a pint. He had a suspicion it was best to wait where he was.

Copley leaned on the bar. He heard the door to the entrance open.

"Copley"

"George"

"The PM will be here in ten minutes. Just wanted to make sure we are both clear what can and can't be said."

"Like Seymour borrowing some bodies off you. George what the hell were you doing messing around with the likes of Thwaites in the first place. You knew of theses bombs, what the fuck do you think you were playing at. Where's Evelyn and Jessica?"

"Evelyn is here. I'm keeping her safe; you have my word I have no idea where Jessica is , nobody has seen them since this morning."
"Keeping Evelyn safe. Evelyn is quite capable of keeping herself safe. Where's my phone and laptop?
"All will be returned to normal once we agree on one or two things.!
"That obviously includes Evelyn. George Gale I expected better of you. Was Thwaites working for you? Was this all some elaborate plot to overthrow the Government?"
"Copley. I assure you it was no such thing. We mislaid the bombs and I had to allow Thwaites to find them discreetly for us."
"Discreetly"
"You let a madman loose"
I know that now."
"You fucking knew. How did you manage to lose thirty nuclear bombs?"
"Copley it wasn't anything to do with me, I only found out a year ago. We were in the dark. Rumours. Nothing to go on."
"Until Thwaites comes up with the goods and then goes loco."
"Yes."

"And you stand there and threaten me to keep quiet. You are a fucking traitor. Yes. Traitor to everything you supposedly hold dear. For a starters Evelyn. Using her as a pawn in your dirty little game. You put the nation at dire risk and for what? Thwaites. I think not. You would have seen through that blustering pathetic fucker. No, There's more to this. You forget I know you George. This isn't the meticulous Government servant George I know. You never lost them. You knew all the time. This was a way of shifting blame, so you and your kind weren't going to be held responsible for the mess. This is the George that throws me into the arms of a barmaid with very unusual tastes. This is the George that has always thought he could manipulate me as a result. You failed then. You didn't learn that I couldn't care less about what people think of my sex life; my ancestry should have told you that; we shagged anything that moved. You couldn't stand it when I got together with Evelyn. You really couldn't believe it. I've seen you look at Evelyn. I've tolerated it, because the other George was a good pal. What happened George? Thirty pieces of silver was it. Your friends at Cambridge? You're working for… "

Copley took a step towards Gale with every intention of hitting him. Gale went for his left inside pocket. At which point Jeff appeared like a jack in the box from behind the bar with a full bottle of whisky winging it and smashing it into Gales face so hard Gale was knocked back onto the floor in a flood of whisky and glass. Copley nearly as shocked as Gale had his foot on Gale's throat before he could regain his sense.

"Where the hell did you come from?"

Gale was groaning. Copley applied a little more pressure.

"Sorry George but you don't threaten me and especially not with Evelyn as your bargaining tool. Now Jeff what do we do with him and how do we get out of here without Georges pals getting suspicious."

"We don't have to worry about his friends. Apart from the Police outside. George has assigned everyone away from here. He wanted nobody here."

"Is the PM coming, or was that just George?"

"No. She's coming. I've been listening to the conversation George was having on the phone. These walls do really have ears and hidden passages."

Why do you think Evelyn and I come here.

"Where's Evelyn and Jessica. Are they ok?"

"George was lying to you. He doesn't have Evelyn, she got us up really early this morning and we walked out of the Inn and up to this old mine cabin; well, underneath the security actually"

"Miterdale Levels."

"Yes. That's right. Evelyn got a message in the night from her German contacts. They eventually worked out all the messages Thwaites was making to Germany, mostly to Erika, but also to George Gale. Gale was in on this from the start."

There was a creaking and the cellar door opened in the floor of the bar

"He was my love"

"Evelyn"

Evelyn pulled herself out of the depths. Followed by Jessica.

"George just sat on it. Pretended it would go away and then when it all got out of hand courtesy of his stooge going mad, he gambled an entire nation on you coming up with a solution. At least that's the version the PM will swallow. What she doesn't know won't make any difference. Before you say why didn't I say anything last night. You were exhausted and if I had you would have gone off on one with George before you sorted Thwaites. It was imperative to deal with Thwaites first"

Evelyn crossed to Copley. Copley was aware the body under his shoe was very still. He did not relieve the pressure. He noted the bottle. A good malt. George enjoyed a good malt. It seemed only appropriate that his last drink was a fine one. Not that he deserved it. Bastard. Copley poured a large measure over Georges head, wetting his own boot.

"There you go. I suppose I should see it as a compliment that he wanted me to tackle this; but consider the death and terror and what if I hadn't stopped the wretched thing. But of course, I did. Now I wonder what possible honour can be bestowed for this act; bugger all if I know the PM?"

Jeff looked down at the whisky blood-soaked body under Copley's boot. It did not look peaceful.

"Copley, I think you can take your boot off now. What are we going to do with the body?"

Jessica looked at her parents then at Jeff.

"Well. We get rid of the fingerprints for a start, I'm not having my boyfriend up on a murder charge. Jeff pass me that dustpan, that bottle neck needs to vanish."

"Jessica. I wouldn't worry too much, I know the PM, decent sort; she's seen worse. Evelyn went to school with her. Didn't you darling. I anticipate a statement along the lines of an unfortunate accident ending with a heart attack. The strain of everything. "Sadly missed. He just slipped away"

Copley looked at Evelyn; he knew Evelyn would sort it. They heard several cars pull up outside. Copley hugged Evelyn. They looked into each other's eyes with a look that surpassed mere passion.

"Sorry I left you to face this one alone"

"Evelyn, you did the right thing. You kept away from George. Kept me facing Thwaites. You always know best, because you know me"

"Copley that's so true."

Jeff stood, somewhat shocked but happy, knowing Jessica had just said "Boyfriend". Copley took it he was worried about the consequence of banjaxing Gale.

"Don't concern yourself Jeff, he will soon be under the sod."

Finis (For Now)

www.ingramcontent.com/pod-product-compliance
Lightning Source LLC
Chambersburg PA
CBHW020114180626
46812CB00006B/2595